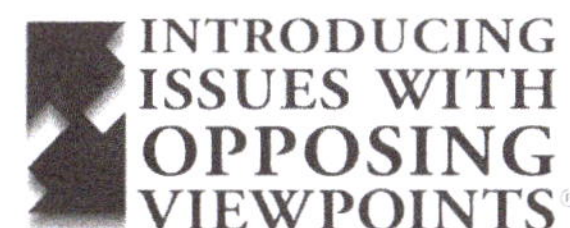

Cults, Sects, and New Religions

M. M. Eboch, Book Editor

Published in 2020 by Greenhaven Publishing, LLC
353 3rd Avenue, Suite 255, New York, NY 10010

First Edition

Articles in Greenhaven Publishing anthologies are often edited for length to meet page requirements. In addition, original titles of these works are changed to clearly present the main thesis and to explicitly indicate the author's opinion. Every effort is made to ensure that Greenhaven Publishing accurately reflects the original intent of the authors. Every effort has been made to trace the owners of the copyrighted material.

Library of Congress Cataloging-in-Publication Data

Names: Eboch, M. M., editor.
Title: Cults, sects, and new religions / M.M. Eboch, book editor.
Description: First Edition. | New York : Greenhaven Publishing, 2020. | Series: Introducing issues with opposing viewpoints | Includes bibliographical references and index. | Audience: Grades 7-12.
Identifiers: LCCN 2019022608 | ISBN 9781534506671 (library binding) | ISBN 9781534506664 (paperback)
Subjects: LCSH: Cults. | Sects.
Classification: LCC BP603 .C85 2020 | DDC 209--dc23
LC record available at https://lccn.loc.gov/2019022608

Manufactured in the United States of America

Website: http://greenhavenpublishing.com

Contents

Foreword 5
Introduction 7

Chapter 1: Why Do People Join Cults and Sects?

1. What Are Cults, Sects, and New Religions? 12
   Irving Hexham
2. It's Not Brainwashing 18
   Rebecca Moore
3. Cults Offer Community 24
   Michael Thomas
4. Cult Mind Control Methods 29
   Cultwatch
5. I Thought a Cult Saved Me, but I Was Wrong 38
   Marye Harrison

Chapter 2: Are Cults and Sects Dangerous?

1. Maybe Cults Aren't That Different from Other Religious Movements 45
   Andrew Singleton
2. Cults Can Offer a Better Life 50
   Ruwan Meepagala
3. Small Religious Groups Are Valid, Too 56
   Christian Assemblies International
4. Cults Are a Danger to College Students 61
   Kate Coxon
5. Prosecute Crimes, but Don't Persecute Religions 67
   Ismatu Ropi

Chapter 3: What Should We Do About Cults and Sects?

1. When Protecting Religion Harms Children 73
   Leah Sottile
2. France Bans Cults to Protect People 80
   Gerry Hadden
3. We Need to Know the Truth About Cults 86
   Eileen Barker

4. Helping People Leave Cults Is a Delicate Operation 93
Rick Ross
5. What to Do When a Loved One Joins a Cult 102
Rod Dubrow-Marshall and Linda Dubrow-Marshall

Facts About Cults, Sects, and New Religions 107
Organizations to Contact 110
For Further Reading 113
Index 117
Picture Credits 120

Foreword

Indulging in a wide spectrum of ideas, beliefs, and perspectives is a critical cornerstone of democracy. After all, it is often debates over differences of opinion, such as whether to legalize abortion, how to treat prisoners, or when to enact the death penalty, that shape our society and drive it forward. Such diversity of thought is frequently regarded as the hallmark of a healthy and civilized culture. As the Reverend Clifford Schutjer of the First Congregational Church in Mansfield, Ohio, declared in a 2001 sermon, "Surrounding oneself with only like-minded people, restricting what we listen to or read only to what we find agreeable is irresponsible. Refusing to entertain doubts once we make up our minds is a subtle but deadly form of arrogance." With this advice in mind, Introducing Issues with Opposing Viewpoints books aim to open readers' minds to the critically divergent views that comprise our world's most important debates.

Introducing Issues with Opposing Viewpoints simplifies for students the enormous and often overwhelming mass of material now available via print and electronic media. Collected in every volume is an array of opinions that captures the essence of a particular controversy or topic. Introducing Issues with Opposing Viewpoints books embody the spirit of nineteenth-century journalist Charles A. Dana's axiom: "Fight for your opinions, but do not believe that they contain the whole truth, or the only truth." Absorbing such contrasting opinions teaches students to analyze the strength of an argument and compare it to its opposition. From this process readers can inform and strengthen their own opinions, or be exposed to new information that will change their minds. Introducing Issues with Opposing Viewpoints is a mosaic of different voices. The authors are statesmen, pundits, academics, journalists, corporations, and ordinary people who have felt compelled to share their experiences and ideas in a public forum. Their words have been collected from newspapers, journals, books, speeches, interviews, and the Internet, the fastest growing body of opinionated material in the world.

Introducing Issues with Opposing Viewpoints shares many of the well-known features of its critically acclaimed parent series, Opposing

Viewpoints. The articles allow readers to absorb and compare divergent perspectives. Active reading questions preface each viewpoint, requiring the student to approach the material thoughtfully and carefully. Photographs, charts, and graphs supplement each article. A thorough introduction provides readers with crucial background on an issue. An annotated bibliography points the reader toward articles, books, and websites that contain additional information on the topic. An appendix of organizations to contact contains a wide variety of charities, nonprofit organizations, political groups, and private enterprises that each hold a position on the issue at hand. Finally, a comprehensive index allows readers to locate content quickly and efficiently.

Introducing Issues with Opposing Viewpoints is also significantly different from Opposing Viewpoints. As the series title implies, its presentation will help introduce students to the concept of opposing viewpoints and learn to use this material to aid in critical writing and debate. The series' four-color, accessible format makes the books attractive and inviting to readers of all levels. In addition, each viewpoint has been carefully edited to maximize a reader's understanding of the content. Short but thorough viewpoints capture the essence of an argument. A substantial, thought-provoking essay question placed at the end of each viewpoint asks the student to further investigate the issues raised in the viewpoint, compare and contrast two authors' arguments, or consider how one might go about forming an opinion on the topic at hand. Each viewpoint contains sidebars that include at-a-glance information and handy statistics. A Facts About section located in the back of the book further supplies students with relevant facts and figures.

Following in the tradition of the Opposing Viewpoints series, Greenhaven Publishing continues to provide readers with invaluable exposure to the controversial issues that shape our world. As John Stuart Mill once wrote: "The only way in which a human being can make some approach to knowing the whole of a subject is by hearing what can be said about it by persons of every variety of opinion and studying all modes in which it can be looked at by every character of mind. No wise man ever acquired his wisdom in any mode but this." It is to this principle that Introducing Issues with Opposing Viewpoints books are dedicated.

Introduction

"Young people are warned about drugs and unprotected sex. But every school-leaver should be taught that a friendly stranger could be the biggest danger they will ever meet."

–Audrey Chaytor of FAIR (Family Action Information and Resource)

Are you in a cult? Would you ever join one?

Can you be sure of your answer?

By some estimates, the United States had thousands of cults. Cults like to recruit on college campuses, where young people may feel lost and alone. A person may join the group because it promises guidance and community. At first, its members are warm and welcoming. Over time, the cult may persuade students to drop out of school and cease contact with their family members and friends. Eventually, the new recruit may discover that the group controls everything they do. The cult tells them what to think and how to feel. Their lives change completely, in ways they never imagined or wanted when they first joined.

Anyone can wind up in a cult, according to many experts. People who join cults can be intelligent and educated. They can be "regular people." After joining the cult, they may seem to undergo a complete personality change. They may do things that go against their previous values. In rare cases, they may kill themselves or others at the command of the cult.

It can be hard to understand why someone would join a cult. It can be hard to even define what a cult is.

Some people prefer the term "new religious movement" because that sounds less judgmental than "cult." A new religious movement may be any small religion that has developed fairly recently. A religious group that departs from the usual accepted standards of religion could be either a sect or a cult. It may be considered a sect if it keeps traditional beliefs and practices but has some specific differences. It may be called a cult if it has beliefs and practices that are farther away from the accepted standards.

To some people, a sect is fine, but a cult is bad. To others, there's no difference.

Some people call Scientology, Jehovah's Witnesses, and Mormonism cults. Yet each of these groups has millions of members and is over one hundred years old. They would not fit the definition of cults as small, new religions. But how small is small enough? How new is new? Every religion started somewhere. At one time, it was small enough to be called a sect or outrageous enough to be called a cult.

Other people call a group a cult if it uses certain "cultish" tactics. Most cultish groups are founded and run by charismatic leaders. Members do whatever the leaders demand and may even worship the leaders before or after their deaths. Cults may use fear, shame, and guilt on members in order to control them. They may punish anyone who tries to leave the group or disagrees with its leaders.

Even nonreligious groups can be called cults. Some business organizations, political groups, self-help groups, or therapy groups are criticized as being cults. Nonreligious groups are most likely to be called cults if they use cult tactics to manipulate members, utilizing the psychologically manipulative tools of cults in nonreligious settings. For example, consider a company that sells health, beauty, and lifestyle products. The company has charismatic leaders and aggressive recruiting techniques. It introduces new recruits to a powerful, exclusive community that it calls a family. The company exerts a great deal of control over sales representatives. For these reasons, this company may be called a cult.

The word "cult" is usually used in a negative way. Extreme examples get the most attention, and people tend to think of Charles Manson, Jonestown, and Branch Davidians when they hear the word "cult." The news shares horror stories about mass suicides or compounds turned into paramilitary bases. Even beyond these worst-case scenarios, cults can do harm. They can break up families. They may pressure people to give all of their money and belongings to the cult. Cults are accused of brainwashing and mind control. Many people hear the term "cult" and assume that anyone in the group must be crazy.

Is this reality or hysteria? The answer depends on whom you ask.

Some experts claim that brainwashing isn't real. Cult behavior can be explained by other psychological insights. Members of new religious movements typically do not feel they are being controlled. They joined the group because it gave them something they needed or because it matched their values. Yet other experts point to the manipulation techniques cults may use. Recruiters may lure people in slowly, hiding many of the realities of the group. Group members may put on a happy face in front of newcomers, regardless of how things are behind the scenes. Once someone has joined, group leaders may use pressure, guilt, and fear to control that person's behavior. When something good happens to a new member, the cult claims responsibility. If something bad happens, the cult blames the member for not working hard enough on the cult's behalf.

Ultimately, it's hard to pin down what defines a cult. Some people may benefit from joining a new religious movement. The group may give them a sense of belonging or help them see the world in a new way. Other recruits may suffer, losing years of their lives to a group that doesn't live up to its promises. Group leaders typically have power, which they may or may not misuse. Members could commit extreme acts due to religious zeal, but any religious movement may demand intense devotion from its followers. In the end, what a person calls a cult may reflect their own beliefs more than the group's.

In some countries, such as France and Indonesia, the government places restrictions on cults. These governments believe they have a right and responsibility to intervene in people's religious beliefs when it puts citizens at risk. They may pass laws against cults in an attempt to protect citizens from terrorism or abuse. Other countries prioritize freedom of religion. The government can only interfere if the group or its members break other laws. In the United States, new religious movements—whether you call them cults or sects or something else—are legal. In some cases, governments even protect small religious groups that break the law. For instance, people who believe in faith healing may refuse to take their children to doctors. In Idaho, faith healing parents cannot be prosecuted for abuse even if their children die for lack of standard medical care.

Cults, sects, and new religions are surrounded by controversy. Are they a danger to individuals and society or simply another means of expressing religious beliefs? What, if anything, should we do about these groups? Should cults be treated differently from sects and new religions? Exploring the issues through research, philosophical discussions, and personal experience can help individuals determine their answers to these questions. The current debates are explored in *Introducing Issues with Opposing Viewpoints: Cults, Sects, and New Religions*, shedding light on this ongoing issue.

Chapter 1

Why Do People Join Cults and Sects?

People join religious or spiritual communities for a wide range of reasons.

What Are Cults, Sects, and New Religions?

"[N]ew religions express a 'love of the new' and rejection of tradition as an authoritative guide for contemporary beliefs and practices."

Irving Hexham

The following viewpoint provides definitions of different types of religious organizations. The author notes that it can be hard to define "religion," as many people have their own interpretations of the word. This makes it equally hard to define "sects" and "cults." One definition asserts that sects and cults are deviant, which here simply means that they depart from the usual, accepted standards. However, sects still keep traditional beliefs and practices, while cults introduce new beliefs and practices. The author notes that the word "cult" has many negative associations. Using a different term can come across as less critical. Irving Hexham is professor of religious studies at the University of Calgary in Alberta, Canada. He is an internationally recognized expert on new religious movements.

"'By Religion I Mean...' Some Possible Definitions Of Cults, New Religions, And Related Groups," Irving Hexham. Reprinted by permission.

AS YOU READ, CONSIDER THE FOLLOWING QUESTIONS:

1. What is the difference between a church, a sect, and a cult?
2. What are revitalization movements?
3. How do new religions and new religious movements relate to cults and sects, according to this viewpoint?

Rodney Stark and William Sims Bainbridge, in (*A Theory of Religion* (New York, Peter Lang, 1987) use the work of sociologist Benton Johnson (1963) to construct a more reliable guide to religious organizations. They define church, sect, and cult as follows:

- A church is a conventional religious organization.
- A sect is a deviant religious organization with traditional beliefs and practices.
- A cult is a deviant religious organization with novel beliefs and practices.

(Stark and Bainbridge 1987:124).

These definitions are precise and for the most part avoid value judgements on the worth of each movement. They also allow for change over time so that what may be a novelty today can become a tradition tomorrow and convention in a hundred years time. Another advantage of them is that they clearly distinguish religious from non-religious organizations. After all not everything is a "religious" phenomenon.

According to Stark and Bainbridge a religion must be based on some "supernatural assumptions" to distinguish it from secular thought. In their view religions involve:

> *"systems of general compensators based on supernatural assumptions" (1987:39).*

By compensators they mean whatever people regard as rewards whether or not they are immediately apparent (1987:36)

Finally, it needs to be noted those groups which Stark and Bainbridge identify as sects and cults can also be seen as revitalization movements (1987:188).

There are thousands of religions practiced aound the world—some estimate as many as 4,200. Religions each have their own sets of beliefs, symbols, and practices. Pictured above are some of the symbols used to represent various religions.

Revitalization movements attempt to revive religious traditions through practical innovations and new expressions of traditional piety. They do not, however, seek to fundamentally change a tradition or incorporate radically new beliefs. Consequently revitalization movements do not produce new religions, rather they reaffirm old traditions.

What Are New Religious Movements?

Despite the wonderfully concise meaning that Stark and Bainbridge assign it, the word cult remains an emotionally loaded term burdened with negative imagery. For this reason many writers have adopted the convention of calling contemporary groups, identified as either cults or sects, new religious movements (NRM's), or new religions.

Unfortunately, redefining cults as new religions can also confuse the issue. For example in Stark and Bainbridge's view cults grow out of established traditions to which they remain attached. In this sense they may be new religious movements, but not new religions. New religions on the other hand break with existing traditions to create something which did not previously exist.

Thus, as a first approximation, we might define new religious movements as cults and sects which although directly related to modernity grow out of existing traditions which are very important sources for their beliefs and practices.

On the other hand new religions are those groups which reject any attachment to clearly identified ongoing traditions. In this sense new religions express a "love of the new" and rejection of tradition as an authoritative guide for contemporary beliefs and practices.

Modernity is more than the spread of industrialization which has still to impact some societies. Rather, it is change brought about by an awareness of industrial goods, science, and technology. Modernity implies a distinction between that which is new as opposed to that which is ancient, or, that which is innovative as opposed to that which is traditional. It is usually an explicit and self-conscious commitment to be "modern" in intellectual, cultural and religious affairs.

How Is *Religion* Defined?

In the *Concise Dictionary of Religion* (Downers Grove, InterVarsity Press, 1993:186-187) Irving Hexham wrote:

> *Hundreds of different definitions of religion exist each reflecting either a scholarly or a dogmatic bias depending in the last resort on the presuppositions of the person making the definition. Religion clearly contains intellectual, ritual, social and ethical elements, bound together by an explicit or implicit belief in the reality of an unseen world, whether this belief be expressed in supernaturalistic or idealistic terms.*

Fast Fact

"Religion" refers to the worship of a supernatural power. It involves the belief in an unseen power and an unseen world. "Secular" refers to attitudes and activities that do not have a religious or spiritual basis.

A number of the more common definitions are:

- Berger, Peter: "the human enterprise by which a sacred cosmos is established."
- Durkheim, Emile: "a unified system of beliefs and practices relative to sacred things."
- Frazer, James: "a propitiation or conciliation of powers superior to man which are believed to direct or control the course of nature and human life."
- Hegel, George: "the knowledge possessed by the finite mind of its nature as absolute mind."
- James, William: "the belief that there is an unseen order, and that our supreme good lies in harmoniously adjusting ourselves thereto."
- Kant, Immanuel: "the recognition of all our duties as divine commands."
- Marx, Karl: "the self-conscious and self-feeling of man who has either not found himself or has already lost himself again... the general theory of the world... its logic in a popular form... its moral sanction, its solemn completion, its universal ground for consolation and justification. It is the fantastic realization of the human essence..."
- Schleiermacher, Friedrich: "a feeling for the infinite" and "a feeling of absolute dependence."
- Stark, Rodney: "any socially organized pattern of beliefs and practices concerning ultimate meaning that assumes the existence of the supernatural."
- Whitehead, Alfred North: "what the individual does with his own solitariness."
- Weber, Max: "to say what it is, is not possible... the essence of religion is not even our concern, as we make it our task to study the conditions and effects of a particular type of social behavior."

The one I find most useful is:

- Smart, Ninian: "a set of institutionalized rituals identified with a tradition and expressing and/or evoking sacral sentiments directed at a divine or trans-divine focus seen in the context of the human phenomenological environment and at least partially described by myths or by myths and doctrines."

EVALUATING THE AUTHOR'S ARGUMENTS:

In this viewpoint, the author explores different definitions of religion, cults, and sects. Why is it so hard to give a single, simple definition? What are the advantages to considering a variety of definitions? Is it possible to entirely avoid making value judgments when creating definitions for different types of religious and spiritual beliefs, or is it impossible to completely remove bias?

It's Not Brainwashing

Rebecca Moore

"Converts begin by being passive recipients of a transcendent, life-changing event."

In the following viewpoint, the author describes how her sisters were drawn into a cult. The author notes that many people assume those who join cults have been brainwashed, but she argues that the term has little basis in science. If brainwashing truly worked, people would never be able to choose to leave cults. She prefers to explore other explanations for cult behavior. She discusses conversion, conditioning, and coercion as explanations for cult behaviors. These practices can even explain why cult members sometimes do things that go against their previous values. Rebecca Moore is a professor emerita of religious studies at San Diego State University.

AS YOU READ, CONSIDER THE FOLLOWING QUESTIONS:

1. What is conversion, as the author describes it?
2. How can conditioning influence people's behavior?
3. How can coercion explain why people may act against their own values?

Nearly 40 years ago, my two sisters, Carolyn Layton and Annie Moore, were among those who planned the mass deaths in Jonestown on Nov. 18, 1978.

Part of a movement called Peoples Temple, which was led by a charismatic pastor named Jim Jones, they had moved with 1,000 other Americans to the South American nation of Guyana in order to create a communal utopia. Under pressure from concerned relatives and the media, however, they implemented a plan of group murder and suicide. Jonestown is remembered in the phrase "drinking the Kool-Aid," because more than 900 people died after drinking poison-laced punch. My two sisters and nephew were among those who died.

In the wake of this tragedy, you might think that I would be amenable to the idea that they had been brainwashed. It would absolve their heinous actions and offer an easy explanation for their behavior.

Many argue that people join "cults"—or "new religious movements," the term scholars prefer—because they've been brainwashed. The thinking goes that they've undergone some sort of programming that allows others to manipulate them against their will.

How else to explain why people become immersed in fringe groups that seem so alien to their previous, more socially acceptable lives? How else to account for the fact that—in some cases—they'll even commit crimes?

But like the word "cult," the term brainwashing seems to only be applied to groups we disapprove of. We don't say that soldiers are brainwashed to kill other people; that's basic training. We don't say that fraternity members are brainwashed to haze their members; that's peer pressure.

As a scholar of religious studies, I'm disheartened by how casually the word "brainwashing" gets thrown around, whether it's used to describe a politician's supporters, or individuals who are devoutly religious.

I reject the idea of brainwashing for three reasons: It is pseudoscientific, ignores research-based explanations for human behavior and dehumanizes people by denying their free will.

The women pictured above are Mennonites, which is a Christian sect primarily based in the United States and Canada. It is one of many sects and new religious movements found in North America.

No Scientific Grounding

Brainwashing is used so frequently to describe religious conversions that it has a certain panache to it, as if it were based in scientific theory.

But brainwashing presents what scientists call an "untestable hypothesis." In order for a theory to be considered scientifically credible, it must be falsifiable; that is, it must be able to be proven incorrect. For example, as soon as things fall up instead of down, we will know that the theory of gravity is false.

Since we cannot really prove that brainwashing does not exist, it fails to meet the standard criteria of the scientific method.

In addition, there seems to be no way to have a conversation about brainwashing: you either accept it or you don't. You can't argue with someone who says "I was brainwashed." But real science seeks argument and disagreement, as scholars challenge their colleagues' theories and presuppositions.

Finally, if brainwashing really existed, more people would join and stay in these groups. But studies have shown that members of new religions generally leave the group within a few years of joining.

Even advocates of brainwashing theories are abandoning the term in the face of such criticism, using more scientific-sounding expressions such as "thought reform" and "coercive persuasion" in its stead.

Conversion, Conditioning and Coercion

Once we move beyond brainwashing as an explanation for people's behaviors, we can actually learn quite a bit about why individuals are drawn to new ideas and alternative religions or make choices at odds with their previous lifestyles.

There are at least three scientific, neutral and precise terms that can replace brainwashing.

The first is "conversion," which describes an individual's striking change in attitude, emotion or viewpoint. It's typically used in the context of religious transformation, but it can describe other radical changes—from voting for the "wrong" candidate to joining Earth First!

It can be sudden and dramatic, as in the case of St. Paul, who had been persecuting the early church but then stopped after supposedly hearing a voice from heaven. Or it can be a slow and gradual process, similar to the way Mahatma Gandhi came to understand his role and mission as a leader for Indian independence.

We usually think of conversion as a voluntary process. But when we look at accounts of well-respected converts—St. Augustine comes to mind—we find exactly what the philosopher William James said we would: Converts begin by being passive recipients of a transcendent, life-changing event. They don't plan for it; it just happens. But they cannot go back to the way things were before their experience.

Next, there's conditioning, which refers to the psychological process of learning to behave in a certain way in response to certain stimuli. As we grow up and experience life, we become conditioned by parents, teachers, friends and society to think and feel in certain predictable ways. We get rewarded for some things we do and punished for others. This influences how we behave. There is nothing evil or nefarious about this process.

Studies have shown that many of the people who seek out new religions may be predisposed or conditioned to finding a group that fosters their worldview.

Fast Fact

According to the BBC, the mass suicide of Peoples Temple cult members at Jonestown resulted in over 900 deaths; 276 of the victims were children.

But what about the nice people who, in rare cases, end up doing terrible things after joining a new religious movement?

Again, the process of conditioning seems to offer some explanation. For example, peer pressure has the powerful ability to condition people to conform to specific roles they are assigned. In the Stanford Prison Experiment, participants were randomly assigned the role of guard and prisoner—with the guards soon becoming abusive and the inmates becoming passive. Meanwhile, deference to authority, which Stanley Milgram studied in his famous 1961 experiment, may encourage people to do what they know is wrong. In the case of Milgram's experiment, participants applied what they believed were electric shocks to individuals, even as they heard simulated screams of pain.

And finally, coercion can also help explain why people may act against their own values, even committing crimes on occasion.

If someone is told to do something—and threatened with physical, emotional or spiritual harm if they don't—it's coercion. Just because someone carries out an order, it doesn't mean they agree with it. Prisoners of war may publicly denounce their home country or claim allegiance to the enemy just to survive. When they are released from captivity, however, they revert to their true beliefs.

In other words, coercion—or exhaustion, or hunger—can make people do things they might not otherwise do. We don't need a theory of thought reform to understand the power of fear.

A Denial of Agency

True believers certainly exist. My sisters fall into that category. They sincerely promoted the cause of the Peoples Temple—no matter how misguided it was under the leadership of Jim Jones—because of their deep commitment to its ideals. This commitment arose from their conversion experiences and their gradual, conditioned acceptance of ethical misbehavior.

I do not consider them brainwashed, however. They made decisions and choices more or less freely. They knew what they were doing. The same is true for members of the Branch Davidians: They accepted and believed the word of God as interpreted by David Koresh.

If brainwashing actually existed, we would expect to see many more dangerous people running around, planning to carry out reprehensible schemes.

Instead, we find that people frequently abandon their beliefs as soon as they leave coercive environments. This fact does not address the difficulty of leaving certain groups, whether they're political parties, religious movements, social clubs or even business organizations.

Nevertheless, people can leave these groups and abandon their beliefs—and do.

Should we consider situational hurdles and peer pressure forms of brainwashing? If that were the case, then everything—and nothing—would constitute mind control.

We have studies that illuminate processes of conversion and conditioning. We have historical examples that demonstrate what people do under compulsion.

The brainwashing explanation ignores this social scientific research. It infantilizes individuals by denying them personal agency and suggesting that they are not responsible for their actions. The courts don't buy brainwashing.

Why should we?

EVALUATING THE AUTHOR'S ARGUMENTS:

In this viewpoint, the author argues that cults do not rely on brainwashing, and that brainwashing does not actually exist. Are her alternate theories convincing? Are they useful in understanding cult behavior? What are the advantages to understanding why people join cults?

Cults Offer Community

Michael Thomas

"People find themselves in a cult having joined a community of people with whom they have come to identify…"

In the following viewpoint, the author explores why people join cults. He says people join groups—including cults—for a sense of community. They may find answers they haven't been able to find elsewhere. Cults may suggest that traditional religion has failed and that they offer an alternative. As examples of cults, the author uses the Jehovah's Witnesses and the Mormons. However, these groups do not fit many widely accepted definitions of cults, as each has millions of members and is over one hundred years old. For Thomas's purposes, cults are religious groups that proactively seek converts. Michael Thomas is a Christian and former Mormon. He is the chairman of Reachout Trust in England. This organization reaches out to cult members and encourages them to return to traditional Christianity.

AS YOU READ, CONSIDER THE FOLLOWING QUESTIONS:

1. Why do cult members reach out to friends, family, and strangers to introduce them to the cult?
2. How might cult members slowly introduce newcomers to their religion?
3. What does the author suggest distinguishes cults from traditional religious belief?

"5 Reasons People Join Cults and Cults Are Successful," by Michael Thomas, Reachouttrust.org, January 5, 2017. Reprinted by permission.

We are frequently asked why people join cults, often with a tone of incredulity. The truth is no one joins a cult. People find themselves in a cult having joined a community of people with whom they have come to identify, a settled community that seems to have answers not found elsewhere. They have been invited, included, taken seriously, treated well, and encouraged.

Cults are proactive in seeking out converts and when they find one they know exactly what they want to do with them. Jehovah's Witnesses will want to visit regularly and do a book study, to get you to the Kingdom Hall, get you integrated into their community.

Mormons will want to spend time with you, to take you through a set of lessons, get you to meet other Mormons, to integrate you into the LDS community. The contact doesn't think of this as an invitation to join a cult. Neither does the cult member think they are doing anything but good. No one joins a cult.

There are five things that stand out as key to gaining people's trust and loyalty, building a conversion experience.

The Invite

Both Mormons and Jehovah's Witnesses have well established outreach programmes. Every Jehovah's Witness, health allowing, is expected to give time to "field work," to knocking doors, or standing in the street with their increasingly familiar literature carts.

While the Mormon Church is known for its army of young missionaries, generations of Mormons have been encouraged to play their part in witnessing. Church president David O McKay, while heading the European Mission (1922-1924), coined the phrase *"every member a missionary"* and it was eventually taken up across the church.

Of course, as with orthodox churches, Cults always have those people with nominal involvement who fail to turn out. But there is no question in anyone's mind about this most fundamental aspect of involvement in their respective organisations. Cults have a membership that takes seriously the call to "*go and make disciples.*"(Mt.28:19)

People often join cults and religious movements for a sense of community. This is one of the reasons why recruitment is a major characteristic of cult behavior.

The Narrative

Both Jehovah's Witnesses and Mormons have a story to tell. For both it is about apostasy in the early church and a swift decline into heresy. Both see the early church councils and the resulting creeds as evidence of confusion born of a falling away from plain and simple truths.

This plays well into the common perception that the church is confusing and irrelevant and the claim is fundamental to Christian cults. For Jehovah's Witnesses the story tells of a restoration of those plain and simple truths through Charles Russell and his early Bible students. For Mormons that restoration of truth and authority came through their founding prophet, Joseph Smith.

Both Mormons and Jehovah's Witnesses are very familiar with their founding story and its development. Philip cried, *"We have found the one Moses wrote about in the law, and about whom the prophets also wrote."* (John 1:45) So cult members want to say, "We have found the way!"

The Purpose

The purpose of all this activity for Jehovah's Witnesses is to gather people into "the truth." For Mormons it's much the same, to offer people "God's great plan of happiness." Convinced of the good in their message and the urgency of the need, they will invite friends and family, neighbours and work colleagues to church events, to do a book study, to meet the missionaries, to discuss further their pressing questions about the purpose of life.

> **FAST FACT**
>
> **"Apostasy" is the abandonment of a religious or political belief. The term may specifically be used to describe a Christian who rejects Christianity. "Heresy" is a belief or opinion that goes against traditional religious beliefs, especially Christian beliefs.**

They are quite certain life has a purpose and simply wish to clear away what they see as the fog of confusion in people's lives and put them on the path to redemption. The woman at the well ran to tell her neighbours, *"Come, see a man who told me everything I ever did. Could this be the Christ?"* (John 4:29) So cult members believe they have found clarity and want to share it with others.

The Doctrine

Mormons and Jehovah's Witnesses have a well rehearsed apologetic for their faith. They will understand it at different levels, from the most basic arguments through to the more complex explanations for what they believe. Most can, however, give an account of themselves at some meaningful level and have a range of resources to hand when they get to the end of their personal knowledge and understanding. Doctrine is high on a cult's list of priorities. Like Paul in Athens (Acts 17), they can, when asked, answer the question *"What do you believe?"*

The Community

Behind the cult's activity is a local community of believers who belong in the story and who will wholeheartedly welcome newcomers into that story. And it is into the story newcomers are invited. It is an invitation to understanding, to involvement, and to commitment. It involves discipleship, development, encouragement, and ownership of the narrative of the faith.

People don't join cults. They join communities that seek them out, give them answers, offer them love, provide purpose and structure for their lives. There are issues with cults, of course, such as doctrinal error, legalism, the control and manipulation that distinguishes the cult.

Reachout exists to warn about these and has not gone soft and interfaith on cults. But the basic principles of invitation, narrative, purpose, doctrine, and community are fundamental to our own Christian faith. How might we better use these to reach the lost, to guard against error, and what will it take for a local church to become effective in equipping its members to share the good news with confidence?

[…]

EVALUATING THE AUTHOR'S ARGUMENTS:

In this viewpoint, the author argues that people don't join cults, but instead join a community. Does seeing a cult as a community rather than a fringe religion make a difference? Does it help you understand the appeal of some cults? How does the author's identification as a former Mormon impact his perspective on cults?

Viewpoint 4

Cult Mind Control Methods

"Beware of thinking that you are immune from cult involvement, the cults have millions of members around the world who once thought they were immune, and to this day still have not realized they are in a cult."

Cultwatch

The following viewpoint warns people against believing they could not be persuaded to join a cult. The viewpoint describes misconceptions about cults and explains how cults work through manipulation. It lists recruiting techniques that cults might use. These can include introducing people to the cult slowly rather than explaining all the group's beliefs upfront. Cult members may use pressure, guilt, and fear to manipulate people. The cult may provide instant friendships, where cult members fake being happy and welcoming. Newcomers may be warned about all the things they will lose if they do not stay with the cult. Cultwatch is an organization that aims to help people trapped in cults and to warn people about the dangers of cults. The organization is made up of people from different Christian denominations.

AS YOU READ, CONSIDER THE FOLLOWING QUESTIONS:

1. How easy is it to identify a cult and cult members, according to the viewpoint?
2. How is "mind control" defined in this viewpoint?
3. How can guilt and love be used to control people?

Cults, wonderful on the outside, but are on the inside very manipulating. Cult leaders are desperate to trick you into joining. They are after your obedience, your time and your money. Cults use sophisticated mind control and recruitment techniques that have been refined over time.

Beware of thinking that you are immune from cult involvement, the cults have millions of members around the world who once thought they were immune, and to this day still have not realized they are in a cult.

To spot a cult you need to know how they work and you need to understand the techniques they use. Teaching you these things is what this article is all about. This article exposes the secret techniques cults will use to try and trick and control you. Cult leaders will not want you to read this, but read it anyway. Once you understand how cults work you will be better able to spot and avoid cult recruiters, and protect your family and friends. First let's eliminate some misconceptions about cults.

Misconceptions About Cults

- Cults are easy to spot, they wear strange clothes and live in communes: Well some do. But most are everyday people like you and me. They live in houses. They wear the same clothes. They eat the same food. Cult leaders don't want you to know that you are being recruited into a cult and so they order their recruiters to dress, talk and act in a way that will put you at ease. One cult has even invented a phrase to describe this, they call it "being relatable".
- Cults are full of the weak, weird and emotionally unstable: Not true. Many cult members are very intelligent, attractive and skilled. The reality is that all sorts of people are involved in cults. One of the few common denominators is that they were often recruited at a low point in their life—more about that later.
- Cults are just a bunch of religious nut cases: This is a common mistake people make thinking that cults are purely religious groups. The modern definition of a mind control cult refers

Cults often recruit members by inviting them to attend meetings, where they can see the group's charismatic leader and enthusiastic, happy members in action. They do this instead of explaining the group's beliefs up front.

to all groups that use mind control and the devious recruiting techniques that this article exposes. The belief system of a religion is often warped to become a container for these techniques, but it is the techniques themselves that make it a cult. In a free society people can believe what they want, but most people would agree that it is wrong for any one to try to trick and control people.

[…]

What Is a Cult?

The modern definition of a mind control cult is any group which employs mind control and deceptive recruiting techniques. In other words cults trick people into joining and coerce them into staying. This is the definition that most people would agree with. Except the cults themselves of course!

[…]

Mind Control

Mind Control is a suite of psychological techniques that cult leaders attempt to control their members with.

Cultwatch does not consider Mind Control to be some magical device which can take away peoples' free will. In other words it does not turn people into some sort of remote control robot. Rather we see Mind Control as a dishonest influence placed covertly on cult members by the cult. So instead of Mind Control being some sort of irresistible force like the aliens in the movies that take over peoples minds, rather it is more like a gun. The cult leader points the Mind Control "gun" at a member and says, "if you leave us then you will lose all of your friends and family," "if you don't conform then you will go to Hell," "if you don't give us money then you will fail in business."

We have broken Mind Control up into a series of techniques that the cults use. Together these techniques make up Mind Control.

Deception

A cult needs to recruit and operate using deception. Why?

Because if people knew their true practices and beliefs beforehand then they would not join. A cult needs to hide the truth from you until they think you are ready to accept it.

For example, imagine if the leader of Heavens Gate cult was open and honest about the group and had said to new recruits, "Join us, wear strange clothes, get castrated and then drink poison!" he would not have had many takers.

A cult will have a slick well-rehearsed Public Relations front which hides what the group is really like. You will hear how they help the poor, or support research, or peace, or the environment. They will tell you how happy you will be in their group (and everyone in the cult will always seem very happy and enthusiastic, mainly because they have been told to act happy and will get in trouble if they don't). But you will not be told what life is really like in the group, nor what they really believe. These things will be introduced to you slowly, one at a time, so you will not notice the gradual change, until eventually you are practicing and believing things which at the start would have caused you to run a mile.

Exclusivism

A normal religious organization would not have any trouble with you moving to another similar organization as long as you stayed in that same religion. Because it is the belief system that matters, not membership in an organization. For example if you were a Christian then you could move from one church to another and still be a Christian.

However cult leaders will tell you can only be "saved" (or can only be successful) in their organization alone. No other organization has the truth, all others miss the mark. So it is not the belief system that decides your future, but it the belief system AND your membership with that particular group.

The cult leaders need to make you believe that there is no where else you can go and still be saved, and if you ever leave the "one true church" then you are going to hell. This is a fear based control mechanism designed to keep you in the cult. It also gives the cult leaders tremendous power over you. If you really believe that leaving the group equals leaving God (or means you are leaving your only chance to succeed in life), then you will obey the cult leaders even when you disagree with them instead of risking being kicked out of the group. Exclusivism is used as a threat, it controls your behavior through fear.

Be very suspicious of any group that claims to be better than all the others. A religious group may say that other groups following the same religion are OK, but they are the ones who have a better grasp of the truth and they are superior to the rest. This is often just a subtle version of exclusivism.

This is one of the practices that cults are often very deceptive about. For example, first off they may give you the impression that they think you are a true Christian, Buddhist or Muslim and it's not until later that their true position is revealed.

Fear and Intimidation

Cult leadership is feared. To disagree with leadership is the same as disagreeing with God. The cult leaders will claim to have direct authority from God to control almost all aspects of your life. If the cult is not a religious group then questioning the leaders or program will still be seen as a sign of rebellion and stupidity.

Guilt, Character Assassination and Breaking Sessions

Guilt will be used to control you. Maybe the reason you're not making money is because you're not "with the programme." Maybe the reason you're not able to convert new recruits is because "your heart is prideful and full of sin." It could never be that the programme isn't working, or those new recruits have valid reasons for not joining. It's always your fault, you are always wrong, and so you must try harder! You will also be made to feel very guilty for disobeying any of the cult's written or unwritten rules.

[...]

Breaking sessions are when one, two or more cult members and leaders attack the character of another person, sometimes for hours on end. Some cults will not stop these sessions until their victim is crying uncontrollably.

Love Bombing and Relationship Control

Cults know that if they can control your relationships then they can control you. Whether we like it or not we are all profoundly affected by those around us. When you first go to a cult they will practice "love bombing," where they arrange instant friends for you. It will seem wonderful, how could such a loving group be wrong! But you soon learn that if you ever disagree with them, or ever leave the cult then you will lose all your new "friends." This unspoken threat influences your actions in the cult. Things that normally would have made you complain will pass by silently because you don't want to be ostracized. Like in an unhealthy relationship love is turned on and off to control.

Cults also try to cut you off from your friends and family because they hate others being able to influence you. A mind control cult will seek to manoeuvre your life so as to maximize your contact with cult members and minimize your contact with people outside the group, especially those who oppose your involvement.

Information Control

Those who control the information control the person. In a mind control cult any information from outside the cult is considered evil, especially if it is opposing the cult. Members are told not to read it or believe it. Only information supplied by the cult is true. One cult labels any information against it as "persecution" or "spiritual pornography," another cult calls it "apostate literature" and will expel you from the group if you are caught with it. Cults train their members to instantly destroy any critical information given to them, and to not even entertain the thought that the information could be true.

Fast Fact

"Exclusivism" means excluding a person or group. In religious terms, inclusivists believe that anyone may be saved. For example, a Christian inclusivist might believe that people of other religions can be saved by Christ if they are good people. An exclusivist may believe that people will only be saved if they follow a specific religion.

Common sense tells us that a person who does not consider all information may make an unbalanced decision. Filtering the information available or trying to discredit it not on the basis of how true it is, but rather on the basis of how it supports the party line, is a common control method used throughout history.

[…]

Cult Recruiting Techniques

Here are some key warning signs that may indicate a cult is trying to recruit you.

- Hyped meetings: Rather than explain to you what the group believes or what their programme is up front, they will instead insist that you can only understand it if you come to a group meeting. There everyone around you will seem so enthusiastic that you will start to think there is something wrong with you. They create an environment where you will feel uncomfortable and the only way to become comfortable is to join them. This is an application of controlled peer pressure.
- Intense unrelenting pressure: They call repeatedly. Meet you on campus or outside your work. Trick you into coming for only an hour and then lead you into a long study, meeting or

talk. They have to keep the pressure on, otherwise you might snap out of the mind control environment they are trying to immerse you in.

- They tell you that they are not a cult: This is a preemptive strike against the warnings from friends and family members which they know will come. In fact some cults go as far to tell you that Satan will try and dissuade you by sending family members and friends to tell you it is a cult. When this tactic is used then often a warped form of logic occurs in the recruits' mind, the "agents of Satan" do come and tell them that it is a cult. So since the group predicted that would happen, the group therefore must true! Basically if any group tells you that they are not a cult, or that some people call them a cult, then for goodness sake find out why!
- Times you are vulnerable.
- Experiential rather than logical.
- Fake friendship.
- End of world pressure.
- Pressure to do crazy things.
- Secret knowledge.

Key Warning Signs

- Single charismatic leader.
- People always seeming constantly happy and enthusiastic. Especially if you discover that they have been told to act that way for the potential new recruits.
- Instant friends.
- If you are told who you can or cannot talk to or associate with.
- They hide what they teach.
- Say they are the only true group, or the best so why go anywhere else.
- Hyped meetings, get you to meetings rather than share with you.
- Experiential rather than logical.
- Asking for money for the next level.
- Some cults travel door to door during times when women are home alone. They, and this is rather sexist, think that women are easier to recruit and once they have the woman then it will be easier to snare the husband or partner.

- Saying that they have to make people pay for it because otherwise they will not appreciate it. This is of course a very silly reason, plenty of people are able to appreciate things which they did not pay for.

Find Out More

The Internet should be your first stop if the group you are interested in or involved with has an international scope. Most of the larger cults will be mentioned by counter-cult organizations like Cultwatch, and commonly many ex-members will have posted their cult involvement stories on the net.

[…]

EVALUATING THE AUTHOR'S ARGUMENTS:

This viewpoint suggests that mind control is a real technique used by cults. How does this differ from Viewpoint 2, where the author argued against the idea of brainwashing? Does one viewpoint make a better case, or are they describing the same thing with different language?

Viewpoint 5

"There's nothing like having the feeling that your voice is being respectfully heard to encourage you to feel more loyalty and affection."

I Thought a Cult Saved Me, but I Was Wrong

Marye Harrison

In the following viewpoint, the author describes her experience with a Buddhist organization. She joined the Buddhist religious group when she was at a desperate point in her life, and the practice of chanting seemed to help improve her life. She later realized that she had been experiencing confirmation bias, which is the tendency to interpret information in a way that supports one's beliefs even if there is no rational connection between the perceived cause and effect. In other words, when good things happened, the cult claimed responsibility, and she believed them. But when bad things happened, the cult said misfortune was her own fault. She hadn't been devout enough and needed to try harder. The author later decided her own confirmation bias fooled her into giving the cult credit for her successes. Marye Harrison is a former member of Soka Gakkai International, a Buddhist religious movement.

"No One Sets out with the Intention of Joining a Cult..." by Marye Harrison, OpenMind, January 12, 2016. Reprinted by permission.

AS YOU READ, CONSIDER THE FOLLOWING QUESTIONS:

1. How can a religious group give people a sense of control over their own lives?
2. How can confirmation bias lead people to believe that a cult is improving their lives?
3. Why would a cult take responsibility for good things that happen to members, but blame the members for bad things that happen to them?

Some years ago, a friend told me about a Buddhist organization she belonged to, called Soka Gakkai International (SGI). I'd been informally studying Buddhism for a couple of years at that point and had attended a couple of sessions at local temples. Nothing resonated with me. When I went to a local SGI meeting for the first time, I couldn't make it past the lobby; there was something creepy and disembodied about the chanting I could hear coming from the main room. I almost ran out of the building.

Well, fast-forward a few years; my marriage had crumbled, and I was living in a city far away from friends, family and a conventional support system. I was under-employed and working for a woman who, to say the least, was a miserable human being. I had reached a point of depression and despair when my friend suggested that I start chanting to change my life. Nothing I had tried thus far had improved things and that, along with her promise that if my life didn't start to turn around very quickly she would stop practicing after more than 30 years with SGI were persuasive. I respected this person, and if someone as skeptical as she was had found something that she believed was effective, it couldn't hurt to try it.

Miraculously, it worked. I chanted for a better job (with a nicer manager) and enough money to cover buying a new set of tires. I chanted for hours, and with all my heart. Within two weeks, I had a job offer working for someone I liked and received enough of a financial windfall that it temporarily bailed me out of the financial problems I was having. I found a local group (SGI is broken out into local Districts, Chapters, Areas and Regions), started attending meetings and, it seemed, life did a complete turnaround. These people

People often join cults or other religious movements when they are at a low point in their life. They seek out support and guidance on how to improve their situation.

were loving and supportive, good friends . . . we chanted together, socialized, went to monthly meetings in the community center. Every small victory was cause for celebration and further encouragement; my setbacks were met with urgings to chant more, study more . . . have more faith that things would work and most importantly make a heart-to-heart with the president of SGI, Daisaku Ikeda. He knew my struggles, and was chanting for me! I wasn't really clear on how 78-year old man in Japan who didn't speak a word of English knew what was going on with me, but apparently he did, so hooray!

This was all extremely seductive. There's nothing like having the feeling that your voice is being respectfully heard to encourage you to feel more loyalty and affection. The idea of finally having control over my life cemented me to the organization; all I had to do was to chant whatever problems I was having would resolve. I was invited to receive my Gohonzon (the magic scroll that would instantly improve my life-condition); I was broke again, but finally saved enough to make my $35.

[…]

I just knew that through the force of my practice and devotion, I could make my life better and, as a result, improve the lives of those around me. That was my personal, self-appointed mission. And, holy cow, I knew it would work! I could just feel with every bone in my body that I had the tools to make that happen.

Confirmation bias—that's an interesting concept. We start doing something differently, and we perceive every positive event in our lives as being directly attributable to that new action. That's how cults work; they provide you with a new tool to handle those challenges in life, and your mind automatically associates that new tool with a successful outcome. You will be surrounded by people who will reinforce that idea; you'll be congratulated and made the center of very positive attention. In my organization, you would be encouraged to share your story at a meeting: there will be others who will take heart from hearing about your experience. They'll chant more, participate more, donate more and try harder to develop a deeper allegiance to the fearless leader. And there was really so much good fortune to share: green lights all the way to work, not being late for a meeting, finding enough change so that you could buy a soda! Once in a while, it would be something meaningful: a better job, a new love, making it through a difficult challenge—you know, things that *never* happen for people who don't chant.

The meetings kept us busy.

[…]

Busy, busy, busy. Keeping us busy served the organization well; we not only didn't have time to associate very much with people outside of the group, those meetings provided additional conditioning opportunities. There's nothing like 20 minutes of chanting to put you into a trance state and keep you highly susceptible.

Oh, but what if despite your best efforts, it doesn't work? What if, despite spending hours chanting in front of your sacred scroll, attending meetings or volunteering your time, you still can't resolve that pesky problem? It's time to go talk with one of your trusted local leaders; you don't discuss it with anyone outside the organization: they won't understand, because what you're doing is so deep and mystical

Fast Fact

Buddhism is the world's fourth-largest religion. Buddhism encompasses a variety of beliefs and practices. They are largely based on the teachings of the Buddha, who was a religious leader born 2,600 years ago in what is now Nepal.

that only other members can get it. They will be kind, but frank. It's obviously your fault. You weren't chanting enough, or with a sincere enough heart. You aren't participating in enough group activities—didn't you miss that study meeting a couple of months ago? You don't donate enough. You aren't devoted enough to the Greatest Mentor Ever. Or you need to work off all of that terrible karma you've accumulated through your many lives. Or maybe (just maybe), you're doing it so right that you are actually bringing all of that negative karma forward so that you can put it behind you and moving into your bright, shiny new life! It's kind of hard not to visualize a great, festering karmic boil there.

While there's quite a bit of sarcasm in this article, it comes from hindsight. While I was in, before I came to my senses, I eagerly swallowed everything this cult organization fed me. The only thing I questioned was the implied divinity of President Ikeda, but I viewed those doubts as a failure on my part. I believed that if I chanted enough, I could overcome anything, achieve any goal. The Mystic Law (the force behind all of this) was on my side, and because of that, I was a special and superior person. It was beyond my comprehension how anybody who was exposed to this wonderful practice didn't see the absolute common sense of it. Cause and effect—you make a good cause and you reap a positive effect. So simple. Physics!

Being in a cult is like a country dance . . . sometimes you advance, sometimes you retreat. Be assured, though, that there is always someone at the head of the room calling the moves and the tune. Some people are incredibly lucky; they get tired of the dance and start seeing just how senseless and abusive it is. I'm one of those very, very fortunate people; it only took me seven years to start seeing what was going on around me—two of the most intelligent people I know had two and three decades of the SGI Shuffle before hearing the flat notes.

EVALUATING THE AUTHOR'S ARGUMENTS:

In this viewpoint, the author discusses confirmation bias. How could confirmation bias affect people in their religious practice and in other aspects of daily life? How can we separate confirmation bias from true cause and effect? Are there circumstances in which a religious group might truly be responsible for good things happening in someone's life? Why or why not?

Chapter 2

Are Cults and Sects Dangerous?

Jim Jones (pictured) *was the leader of the Peoples Temple, an American cult. In 1978, approximately nine hundred members died in a mass suicide, including Jones.*

Maybe Cults Aren't That Different from Other Religious Movements

Andrew Singleton

"The leadership seeks to exercise great control in their everyday lives — and will use bullying, confession and shaming to obtain and then retain that control."

In the following viewpoint, the author notes that normal people may join cults. Despite misconceptions, cult members often are not poor or uneducated. He then explores the question of how to define a cult. He suggests that cult leaders exert extreme control over the membership. Does this make Scientology a cult, as some claim? It fits the criteria in some ways. But the author notes that any religious movement can require intense devotion and commitment. Leaders can misuse their power, and members can commit extreme acts through religious zeal. Andrew Singleton is a sociologist at Deakin University in Australia. His research includes new religious movements, youth religion, and personal belief.

"What's the difference between a religion and a cult?" by Andrew Singleton, The Wheeler Centre, September 28, 2016. Reprinted by permission.

AS YOU READ, CONSIDER THE FOLLOWING QUESTIONS:

1. What does the author consider to be the era when new religious movements became increasingly common? What are some of the religious movements that arose at that time?
2. How can the behaviors of a religious group's leaders possibly identify a cult, according to the viewpoint?
3. In what ways can a cult be like any other religious movement, according to the author?

When I was younger, some friends of mine joined an apparent cult. They were a church-going couple who got invited to join a local "fellowship," a group that held weekly bible meetings and talked a lot about "holiness." Nothing too unusual; lots of Christians attend bible studies and small fellowship groups during the week. Almost overnight, however, members of this fellowship left their own churches and effectively took over another. Some of them shunned their friends, and in some cases, family members. Word soon got out about semi-arranged marriages, financial control and indoctrination.

This didn't happen in some rural part of Texas, or a remote corner of Victorian countryside. There was no compound ringed with barbed wire, and no suicide pact. This all took place in the leafy eastern suburbs of Melbourne—among doctors, lawyers and stockbrokers. Growing up in that part of the world, I knew quite a few of them. What struck me was how normal they were. Regular people, I realised, could fall prey to a cult.

Cults are in the news again, thanks in part to journalist Louis Theroux's new film, *My Scientology Movie*, and the 2015 documentary, *Going Clear*, both of which offer an exposé of the inner workings of Scientology, a religion founded in America in the 1950s. In *Going Clear*, some former members grimly describe Scientology as a cult. Both films, and their combined impact, constitute a monumental setback for Scientology—a religion that has long strived for adherents, legitimacy and cultural relevance. It has fought various battles across the world for legal recognition, a right Australia's High Court afforded in 1983.

The Church of Scientology pictured is located in Los Angeles, California, which is the city with the highest concentration of Scientology-related organizations. Though legally recognized as a religion in some countries, its status is a source of controversy in others.

Scholars of religion treat Scientology mainly as a "new religious movement" (NRM), one of many to emerge in America over the past 200 years. (Some other notable examples include Pentecostalism, Jehovah's Witnesses, Christian Science, Spiritualism and Mormonism.) Each of these offered new metaphysical revelations, or proclaimed different insights into the human condition. Most had a charismatic leader preaching the radical new message. All of them sat outside the religious orthodoxy of the age and were deeply controversial; now they are an established part of America's vibrant religious mosaic.

As for Scientology being a cult? Scientology is not the first 20th-century NRM to be accused of cult-like conduct. Fuelled by the mood of counter-culture, there was something of a "spiritual awakening" in the mid to late 1960s, and many small movements arose on the fringes of mainstream religion, including the Krishna Consciousness Society (the Hare Krishnas), Eckankar, the Jesus Movement, the Unification Church (the Moonies), Satanism and the Sri Chinmoy movement, among many others. Scientology presaged these, but enjoyed a boom in membership.

Fast Fact

Scientology was founded in America in 1952 by the author L. Ron Hubbard. Followers undertake training in pursuit of self-knowledge and spiritual fulfillment. Many members say the church is about self-improvement. However, medical and scientific groups have criticized its practices.

Bearing witness to these kinds of NRMs, scholars at the time sought to elucidate the hallmarks of a cult, and how they differ from ordinary new religions or breakaway sects. Most agreed that cults were transient movements that rose rapidly and then disappeared quickly.

Arguably, the distinguishing features of a cult lie in the experience of rank-and-file followers. The leadership seeks to exercise great control in their everyday lives—and will use bullying, confession and shaming to obtain and then retain that control. Leaders will exert that control right into personal decisions like who to marry, where to work, or what to wear. Most often, the leadership is not subject to the same scrutiny, or enjoys special privileges, such as commanding sex from followers.

Members are also subject to intense indoctrination—they're told not only that the group's teachings are right, but also that only cult members are chosen to be in possession of these teachings. Those who disagree or threaten the movement are not just apostates, but figures of danger to be shunned. This sometimes leads to family splits, with estrangement between spouses or children from their parents. Given how a cult wraps up a person's life, those who leave have much to lose.

Consequently, participation comes at great cost; financial and emotional. In the most extreme cases, people die, as was the case with infamous cults like the Branch Davidians in Waco, the People's Temple in Guyana, or Heaven's Gate in San Diego. And as I found out when people I knew joined one, those who fall in with a cult are not necessarily more susceptible to "brainwashing," nor are they necessarily impoverished, uneducated or desperate. People convert for all sorts of reasons. It can be something prosaic like an employment opportunity, or because of family or friendship connections. Few people willingly walk into a cult knowing it is a cult—let alone imagine what is in store for them.

Based on the accounts of those who have disentangled themselves from Scientology's inner sanctum in Los Angeles (the "Sea Org"), much of what occurs seems cult-like, as members follow a leader accused of excessive and controlling behaviour. Those in the inner sanctum aggressively target former members who speak out against Scientology.

Yet for rank-and-file members in Melbourne or Johannesburg, the experience of Scientology might be like that of any other religious movement or sect that demands intense devotion and deep commitment from its members. Indeed, much of what Scientology exhibits is not unlike other "strict" religious sects. Every religion—or political ideology—has within it the capacity to foster uncritical zeal, or has the potential for the leadership to misuse their privileged position. As Bruce Springsteen once said, "Blind faith in your leaders, or in anything, [can] get you killed."

EVALUATING THE AUTHOR'S ARGUMENTS:

In this viewpoint, the author suggests that any religious movement can require devotion, strict behavior, and an extreme viewpoint. Is there any point to identifying cults as distinctive from other religions? If so, what criteria can we use? What is the advantage to identifying a group as a cult?

Viewpoint 2

Cults Can Offer a Better Life

"We're constantly getting invitations for potential reality upgrades: advertising, politicians' spiel, self help books, blog articles..."

Ruwan Meepagala

In this viewpoint, the author applies the term "cult" to movements that may not be religious. He says a cult is not always a bad thing—it can lead to a better way of seeing the world. Yet two cults that approached him failed to recruit him because they used poor sales techniques. He then discusses five principles that can help a cult recruit people. He says a cult should first appear to agree with the person they're trying to recruit, which allows people to change their views without embarrassment. The cult offers a better option by showcasing cult members who seem happy and successful. Finally, the cult must be willing to walk away from the new recruit, and it must truly believe it is doing good work. Ruwan Meepagala is self-employed as a life coach.

AS YOU READ, CONSIDER THE FOLLOWING QUESTIONS:

1. Why would a cult point out a potential new member's insecurity, according to the author?
2. Why do cults often recruit using happy, enthusiastic members?
3. Why is a cult more successful if its members truly believe in the cult, according to the author?

"How to Get People to Join Your Cult," by Ruwan Meepagala, betterhumans.coach.me, November 27, 2017. Reprinted by permission.

I was recently contacted by two people from two different cults to have me join them.

I listened to their spiels attentively—because I had been there before.

In my early twenties I was involved with a cult with a health and wellness business as its storefront. While I witnessed many undesirable things, there were many positives and it did in fact usher me in to a more desirable way of seeing the world—what I would call a reality upgrade.

So I listened to two cult members who approached me.

One was from the Flat Earth Society. The other was from a popular personal development organization that descended from a cult in the 70's. I wanted to understand their reality.

And I became irritated. Not because of their worldviews, and not because they were "selling" me. But because they were doing it sloppily…

We're constantly getting invitations for potential reality upgrades: advertising, politicians' spiel, self help books, blog articles…

They are all mild forms of brainwashing (brainrinsing?) and many can positively impact our lives.

You may never call your movement/company/ideology a 'cult.' (No one does.) But if you offer people a new way of perceiving reality, I'm sorry to break it you… it is.

Or at least it functions as one. And that's not a bad thing.

Anytime people agree on a perspective they co-create a reality—hopefully a better one. If you truly does have a better way of seeing the world, I want you to enroll people in your ways.

Here are 5 principles that will help you enroll people into your way of thinking. They worked on me to join a literal cult. I hope you use them for good, not evil.

Validate My Current Observations, Then Offer an Alternate Explanation That Includes It

I did this a lot with Pickup Artists on why to they should take a workshop on empathy. Instead of sh***ing on their misogynistic assumptions (i.e. "all women are shallow" etc.) I told them, "yeah,

Manipulation is often a characteristic of cults and cultlike groups, but it can also be found in many other aspects of life, such as sales and advertising.

you're right, they do seem to be shallow… in situations where their emotional needs aren't being met. Now if you just could learn how to feel what's under that Resting B**ch Face…"

Islam did this with absorbing Jesus as a prophet. Galileo did this with his earlier discoveries under church supervision. Trump kind of did this with underemployment of white males.

It allows the enrollee to save face in adopting a new belief system.

The Flat Earther straight up told me "you're living a lie." Bad move. Even if she was able to convince me the Earth was flat, I'd be embarrassed to 180 my stance.

No one with an ego "changes their mind." We make NEW decisions based on new information.

Highlight My Insecurity

Even though I'm avoiding ethics, this is what makes me most uncomfortable about marketing. (Which is probably why I'm not great at marketing myself.) Mainly because my spiritual belief is that we're all perfect and life is perfect and we're incarnated to entertain our consciousness via the ups and downs of life.

But I do know I would have missed out on a lot of desired experiences if it wasn't for my perception that I NEEDED to do them. A little fear has always helped me overcome complacency.

I WANTED to have a Marines adventure. But I would have never went to OCS (like bootcamp) if my recruiter didn't expose my insecurity about my masculinity.

I WANTED to have an entrepreneurial adventure. But I would have never left corporate work if I wasn't afraid of becoming Willy Loman.

I WANTED to have a cult adventure. But I wouldn't have left my fairly comfortable life if I wasn't having trouble expressing myself.

Few people take action for an incremental improvement. But everyone wants to fix what's broken.

Show Me What I'll Become If I Follow You

This should be obvious as this is basically the purpose of Instagram.

I asked the Flat Earther "how is your life different now that you know the Earth is flat?"

At this point she got "triggered." (Her word, not mine.) Which made me sad because I really wanted to believe that at least she was happy in her fantasy. I would hope that if you're going to dismiss physics you at least have something to show for it…

When I joined my cult, I was mainly attracted by the fact all the teachers were super vibrant, totally self-expressed, bad*ss, and intense AF. Even though not everything they said made sense, *I was willing to suspend disbelief* because they represented what I wanted to be. (Similar to Cialdini's "Halo Effect.")

I later found that much of it was theatrics, but one could argue the ends justifies the means… Again, this isn't a post about ethics, it's a post about truth. If you're going to win me over, you better show me a greener pasture and redder roses (even if your minions had to paint them.)

Be Willing to Drop Me

We only want to follower leaders who don't need us. We're only sexually attracted to people who have other options. We're only willing

Fast Fact

The "halo effect" is when you observe a characteristic in someone and let that single characteristic define your impression of him or her, ignoring any evidence to the contrary. This phenomenon is often used in sales and marketing.

to carry the flag for a general who can replace us if we go down.

In my cult we were taught to "only want for people as much as they want for themselves." That's a brainwash-y line, I know. But the practical meaning is that if someone isn't interested, move on.

Trump: The Art of the Deal lists this as a major rule: Be willing to walk away.

If I get a sense that you NEED me to hit your sales quota (or much worse, to get validation) you're not getting any of my time, money, or attention.

I want to know that if I don't take your "red pill" now, you'll give to the next One. (That analogy has totally ruined the Matrix for me btw.)

Group attachment works on scarcity.

A couple times when I felt "done" with my cult, I stuck around for another cycle because I got the sense I'd get replaced in my role (kind of a reverse FOMO.)

Really Care

If you believe the absolute that "cult" = "evil" this might be confusing. But in my experience, most effective cult enrollers genuinely care and believe they are doing the best for their marks.

The people who enrolled me showed an active interest in my life. My cult mentor (I believe) was truly interested in my enlightenment… Only her understanding of enlightenment was distorted from her own brainwashing.

I helped people totally uproot their lives because I really really believed it was the best thing for them. (Usually it was, but I'm not perfect.) I knew what it was like to be tortured by mediocrity and wanted more than anything to give them a chance out.

The people who reached out to me didn't seem to care about where I was at in life. They couldn't possibly know if they could actually help me, so I didn't believe them when they told me so.

You might not have a literal cult (hopefully), but these are major principles that allow people to follow you. Cults are simply extreme examples of how people naturally organize around ideas.

Your "cult," be it an explicit group or way of thinking, will attract more people if it follows this principles. Just please, don't serve Kool Aid.

EVALUATING THE AUTHOR'S ARGUMENTS:

In this viewpoint, the author says that a cult is not a bad thing if it leads to a better way of seeing the world. What evidence does he present to support this view? Other viewpoints suggests that people don't know what they're getting into when they join a cult. Can a newcomer judge where the cult will take them? If so, how? Does it seem better to carefully judge each group or to avoid anything cultlike?

Small Religious Groups Are Valid, Too

Christian Assemblies International

"[D]oes wrong become right simply by gaining a significant number of followers?"

The following viewpoint explores the meaning of the word "sect." It notes that the term may come across as negative but argues that it simply refers to a smaller religious group. They may follow a large religious movement, such as Christianity, but with slight differences in belief and practice. The viewpoint argues that early Christian groups fit the definition of sect when they were founded. In addition, if size defines a sect, then some groups grow out of being sects. The viewpoint then suggests different criteria for identifying a group as Christian versus a sect. Christian Assemblies International describes itself as a Pentecostal church with an international focus.

AS YOU READ, CONSIDER THE FOLLOWING QUESTIONS:

1. What are the differences between the three types of sects outlined in this viewpoint: aggressive, tolerated, and assimilating?
2. If a group slightly differs from a mainstream religion in practices and beliefs, should it be considered a cult, according to the viewpoint?
3. Whose definition of a sect is being challenged in this viewpoint?

Mormonism is a notable new religious movement that has emerged in the United States. The Book of Mormon is the sacred text for Mormons, and it was first published in 1830.

The terms "sect" and "sectarianism" are applied in the religious, philosophical and the political realms. When we hear these terms we begin to have negative feelings. Nobody wants to be a sectarian, and nobody wants to belong to a sect.

However, the meaning of the word "sect" is not slanderous at all.

The word derives from the Latin secta meaning "followed principle, guideline and party". The Latin noun (according to 'Duden's German dictionary') probably belongs to the Latin sequi (secutum), which means "to follow". The noun "sectarian"—follower of a sect—first appears in the 17th century. It is interesting to note the connection between the words "sequi" and "con-sequent" (in Latin con-sequi—"follow together"). Most common dictionaries explain the term "sect" in the religious realm, as a small fellowship, separated from a Christian church or other main religions.

Christian publications deal in more detail with the term "sect." For example, amongst other things, P. Honigseim writes on page 1657 of "Religion: Past and Present":

"A sect is a structure which is primarily related to religion and has the following features: small in number, it stands next to a comprehensive structure; the members consider themselves to be elite; they have close fellowship; they adhere to special differences that often seem to be rather minor; they assimilate slower (take more time to move into surrounding groups and fellowships [editors note]); and might suffer persecution, detention or loss of reputation. The leadership is less bureaucratic and more charismatic (led by God's Spirit, or by whatever they consider to be God's Spirit [editors note])."

Honigseim compares the sects with the church. He divides them into three main types of sects: the "aggressive sect", the "tolerated sect" and the "assimilating sect." The first one has a striking militant appearance, whereas the second one "denies violence and exists unrecognised." The "assimilating sect" gives in to the pressures of the environment and makes concessions. All sects can end, or scatter, after the death of their founder. The "aggressive sect" is often persecuted and greatly decimated. The remainder then approaches another type. A sect ceases to be a sect when, for example, members practising another way of life join, and concessions are made, or when one gives in and adjusts to the environmental pressures.

R. Mayer states that, according to Protestant church law, sects are "special religious fellowships, which deviate from national and free churches in fundamental points." They are not churches in the sense of the ecclesia visibilis universalis (the universal, visible church), but are "basically, within the Christian realm." (Religion: Past and Present, page 1662).

Some Bible translations use the word "sect" for the Greek hairesis, e.g. Luther in his "1545 Biblia Germanica," in ACTS 5:1; ACTS 15:5; ACTS 24:5, etc.

When we read the definition above, various questions arise:

1. Do we have the right to call a minority a "sect"? Where are the boundaries?
2. After reading the above definition, are "sects" really objectionable? When we think of the beginnings of the Reformation; of the Catharists and Albigenses; the Hussites and Huguenots; even of the beginnings of Christianity; then they would also fit that definition. Furthermore, is it not important for every Christian to hold on to their principles, and to defend the

truth, if necessary at the risk of freedom and life? ("You can take away the body, possessions, honour, wife and child, etc... but you cannot take this away.")

Think about the time of the "religious wars" during the Hitler era. Who decides which differences in teaching are "only minor" for the individual?

FAST FACT

Christian Assemblies International has been investigated for abuses, including physical, sexual, and psychological abuse. In 2018, the group changed leadership and admitted to past wrongdoing.

3. The definition states that sects are groups, small in number. However, we know that, for instance, the Jehovah's Witnesses, the Mormons, etc. have a large membership. Therefore, does wrong become right simply by gaining a significant number of followers?

We need other criteria. Therefore, I suggest testing a fellowship which purports to be "Christian" according to the following points:

1. Do they preach the JESUS of the Bible? (1 JOHN 4:1-3)
2. Do they acknowledge Him as LORD? (1 CORINTHIANS 12:3)
3. Do they add something to salvation through Jesus, which they also consider to be necessary? (ROMANS 3:28; GALATIANS 1:9)
4. Do they accept the Bible as God's Word? Do they believe that the Bible is right on any questions of doubt, as long as we understand it correctly?
5. Do they listen to advice, or do they consider their fellowship to be without mistakes?
6. Do they accept that other fellowships can also be true followers according to the judgment of God, or do they consider it necessary to be a member of their group for salvation, and therefore deprive everybody else of it? Do they accuse us of lack of obedience, of improper imitation of Christ, or of having no authority...?

If all these questions can be answered in a positive way, we must not speak of a "sect." Differences in knowledge will appear time and again. We may not be able and be prepared to personally identify ourselves with certain teachings; nevertheless, we acknowledge our brothers. It may be that it is our duty to point out to them certain dangers and errors and therefore serve them according to JAMES 5:19-20 and JUDE 23.

However, it is different with somebody who: "...transgresseth, and abideth not in the doctrine of Christ..."(2 JOHN 9). Scripture says of him: "receive him not into your house, neither bid him God speed:" (2 JOHN 10).

Our time requires special vigilance. We need useful criteria and we can find them in God's Word.

EVALUATING THE AUTHOR'S ARGUMENTS:

In this viewpoint, a small religious group argues that if a group follows the basic beliefs of a larger religion, it should be included as part of that religion. Do you agree with the group's proposed definition of a sect? Does it matter if a small religious group has some practices that differ from the larger religion? Why or why not? How might the fact that the authors belong to a small religious group themselves impact their motivations for redefining sects?

Cults Are a Danger to College Students

Kate Coxon

> *"Students are especially vulnerable to being recruited because of their stage in life."*

In the following viewpoint, the author notes the prevalence of cult recruitment on college campuses. They appeal to cults for various reasons: many people are gathered in a small area; young people are on their own for the first time and are exploring the world; they may be more open to new ideas about how to live their lives. A group that offers a sense of belonging can appeal to someone who is lonely after leaving their family and friends. Once interested, the student recruit may then be asked to give money to the cult. Some young people even drop out of school to spend more time with the cult. Family members may not recognize what is happening, and when parents find out that their child has joined a cult, it may be too late to interfere. Kate Coxon is a journliast who has written for the *Guardian*, a British daily newspaper.

"Cult following," by Kate Coxon, Guardian News and Media Limited, November 6, 2001. Reprinted by permission.

AS YOU READ, CONSIDER THE FOLLOWING QUESTIONS:

1. Why do cults like to recruit on college campuses?
2. Why are college students especially likely to join a cult?
3. Why can it take family and friends longer to notice a personality change when a college student joins a cult?

Are you young, of above average intelligence, from an economically advantaged background, well educated and idealistic? If you answered yes to the above, you may well be a student. But you also fit the bill for recruitment into a cult.

"To define a cult we use five characteristics, the most important of which is the use of mind-control techniques to recruit people," says Ian Howorth of the Cult Information Centre. "Although cults recruit people of all ages, students—who are intelligent and often intellectually or spiritually curious—are prime targets."

Some disagree with this definition. The Information Network Focus on Religious Movements (Inform), an organisation that aims to offer objective information on religious groups, believes the term "cult" is value-laden and prefers the expression "new religious movements."

Liz Carnelley, chaplain to the universities of Manchester, points out that "one person's cult may be another person's strong religion."

Nevertheless, first-time students, keen to meet others and make friends, tend to be open to new ideas and experiences. This is actively exploited by some groups on the look-out for new members. One organisation, the International Church of Christ, describes campus evangelism as "the goose that laid the golden egg." In its manual, Shining Like Stars, it states that halls of residence are the Christians' evangelistic paradise: "They provide the best environment imaginable for seeking and saving the lost."

The manual offers advice on how to maximise recruitment at mealtimes ("superb evangelistic opportunities") and lectures (inviting the lecturer to church is suggested). Members are urged: "Never again will there be such easy access to so many people on a consistent basis."

The International Church of Christ has been banned from some campuses. Kate Bassett, speaking on behalf of Birmingham University —where the organisation is banned from actively recruiting or

Exploring new communities and beliefs is a common characteristic of college life, but for this reason college students are also prime targets for cult recruiters. Some colleges and universities have banned recruitment on campus to prevent this.

promoting itself on campus—says: "This is a place of academic freedom, but we have a duty of care to our students and staff and we therefore ban groups where we feel that any organisation could harass students or members of staff."

Adrian Hill, spokesperson for the London Church of Christ, denies that students are targeted or harassed. "We don't target anybody we evangelise everybody. We're encouraging people to be gregarious, friendly and great human beings, and to take the opportunity to invite someone else to church.

"We're very excited about what we've got. We want to recreate the church of the first century in the 21st century. We're not aware that we've been banned from anywhere, and if we are, I'd love to hear about it."

The Reverend Andrew Taylor, Anglican chaplain at Royal Holloway College, London University, believes that access to students is an issue of concern: "Religious groups may come on to a campus uninvited in the way that no other individuals would dare in these days of higher security. The church is meant to be inclusive and welcoming, and this aspect is easily abused."

However, religion is not always the hook. The Cult Information Centre reports that "therapy" or "personal development" groups, which may have a slicker, more corporate approach, are increasingly giving cause for concern.

Audrey Chaytor of Fair (Family Action Information and Resource), an organisation that supports families and individuals who have been hurt by cult involvement, estimates that up to half of the calls she receives are from families of students. She believes that the problem is getting worse. "New groups seem to be setting up all the time and it tends to be more of a problem in the bigger cities.

"Students are especially vulnerable to being recruited because of their stage in life. All people in transit—those moving to a new place to study or to work, as well as those on holiday or travelling—are vulnerable, because if someone talks to them they will stop and listen."

Ian Howorth says that when the average person is recruited into a cult, they undergo a drastic personality change. "With new students, it may take longer for family and friends to notice and fully understand the change. Parents may put the change down to leaving home and meeting a new crowd, and by the time they have realised what has happened, it's too late."

For those recruited into some groups, targeting others and "fund-raising" for the cause can become a full-time activity. Reports of students being asked to apply for personal loans with banks or loan sharks are not uncommon.

One parent whose son was recruited into a cult found out only when his bank contacted her about the five-figure debt he had run up within his first two terms. Students may give up their studies in pursuit of a greater cause and lose touch with friends and family.

Cults use many ploys to recruit the unsuspecting. The National Union of Students, which works with the Cult Information Centre to disseminate information on cults to student unions, advises students to be wary of invitations to meetings or lectures where the objectives are not clearly stated.

Chaytor believes that students and parents should be better informed about cults. "Young people are warned about drugs and unprotected sex. But every school-leaver should be taught that a friendly stranger could be the biggest danger they will ever meet," she says.

In the words of one former cult member: "It is so easy to get into a cult —but an absolute nightmare to get out again."

FAST FACT

U. Magazine asked readers about cults on campuses. Forty percent of respondents said cults were active on their college campuses. Seventeen percent said they had been members of a cult on campus at some point. Of those people, almost a quarter said they felt pressured into joining. Thirty-five percent thought the group used mind games to control them.

The Scientologist: A Parent's Story

Peter, 19 (not his real name), was recruited into the Church of Scientology aged 18 during his first year at Birmingham University. His mother gives her account.

"Peter was stopped in the street in his first term and asked to complete a so-called personality test which, as far as I can tell, seems to ask a lot about parental income and employment without actually mentioning Scientology. He had nothing better to do and I believe he felt lonely. He was vulnerable—he had barely turned 18, which is very young. He'd come from a public-school background, with a strong network of friends and, in retrospect, he was probably not streetwise.

"As soon as he joined we noticed an enormous personality change. His language changed—he repeats what must be key group words. He dropped out at the end of his first year and says he is working for them. We have no idea what he does, or where he lives, except that he claims to earn £70 for a full-time working week.

"As he's over 18 there is nothing we can do, except try to keep in contact with him and hope that he manages to come out and finish his degree. Parents and students should be warned about this kind of thing—forewarned is forearmed."

Graeme Wilson, director of public affairs for the UK Church of Scientology, says:

> *"The personality test is an analysis of how you view yourself and simply establishes the areas in life a person wants to improve, if any. Scientologists do tell others about the benefits to be had from Scientology, for the simple reason that these*

solutions work. This is, after all, still a free country and Christians have been spreading the word for over 2,000 years, as have people of most religions.

Many people are walking around asleep: Scientology wakes them up and puts them in control of their lives. It is a very practical religion and I believe it is better for students to get into religion—any religion—than drugs and excessive alcohol. And people do drop out of university routinely and for all manner of reasons.

There is a lot of inaccurate propaganda about Scientology, and some people make a living from stirring up fear and inciting religious hatred—fortunately this will soon become a criminal offence.

But if anyone is upset that a loved one has joined our church we invite them to get in touch with us so we can answer their questions and respond to their concerns."

EVALUATING THE AUTHOR'S ARGUMENTS:

This viewpoint notes that some colleges and universities ban cults from any activity on campus. Given the sources quoted, does that seem like a reasonable way to protect students, or should students be allowed to explore their beliefs without interference? Why do you think this?

Viewpoint 5

Prosecute Crimes, but Don't Persecute Religions

"In dealing with new religious movements, the government should investigate whether a movement has the potential to jeopardise public order before taking action against it."

Ismatu Ropi

In the following viewpoint, the author discusses cults in Indonesia. He uses the term "new religious movements," which is considered less judgmental. He notes that some groups can be peaceful, while others can turn to violence. People also commit violence against religious sects, as demonstrated by an incident in which a mob burned down the homes of members of an Indonesian religious sect called Gafatar. In some countries, such as Indonesia, the government may ban new religious movements even though they are peaceful. In the author's view, those who commit crimes should be brought to justice. However, governments should guarantee religious freedom to everyone. Dr. Ismatu Ropi is a senior researcher at the Center for the Study of Islam and Society. He also teaches at Syarif Hidayatullah State Islamic University in Indonesia.

"How should Indonesia deal with emerging religious cults?" by Ismatu Ropi, The Conversation, March 7, 2016. https://theconversation.com/how-should-indonesia-deal-with-emerging-religious-cults-54464.

AS YOU READ, CONSIDER THE FOLLOWING QUESTIONS:

1. How can political instability lead people to join cults?
2. According to the author, what conditions should exist for a government to ban a religious group?
3. How can banning religious groups lead to more being founded?

In a small regency in West Kalimantan, Indonesia, more than 1000 members of a new religious sect called Gafatar have set up a commune over the past year. Most of them, including a general practitioner who was reported missing in late December with her daughter, have moved from Java in the past year.

In late January, a mob attacked and burned down their houses. Human rights activists condemned the attack and called for the government to protect Gafatar members.

But a lot of people in Indonesia, the world's most populous Muslim country, were also puzzled by the news that young professionals were joining a cult that reportedly mixes elements of Islam, Christianity and Judaism.

Gafatar falls into what religious scholars call "new religious movements." Why and how do such movements emerge? And how should the government deal with emerging religious cults while ensuring religious freedom of all citizens?

New Religious Movements

New religious movements, such as Gafatar, usually fit these criteria:

- are a collective with a charismatic leader;
- actively yet discreetly recruit new members;
- have a hierarchical structure similar to a traditional religion;
- have a religious doctrine that tends to be different from conventional religions; and
- isolate themselves from mainstream society by building a new life order (as Gafatar has done by moving to Mempawah).

Some experts view these movements as representing new interpretations of established religions. Other researchers see it as a response to disillusionment with social and political conditions.

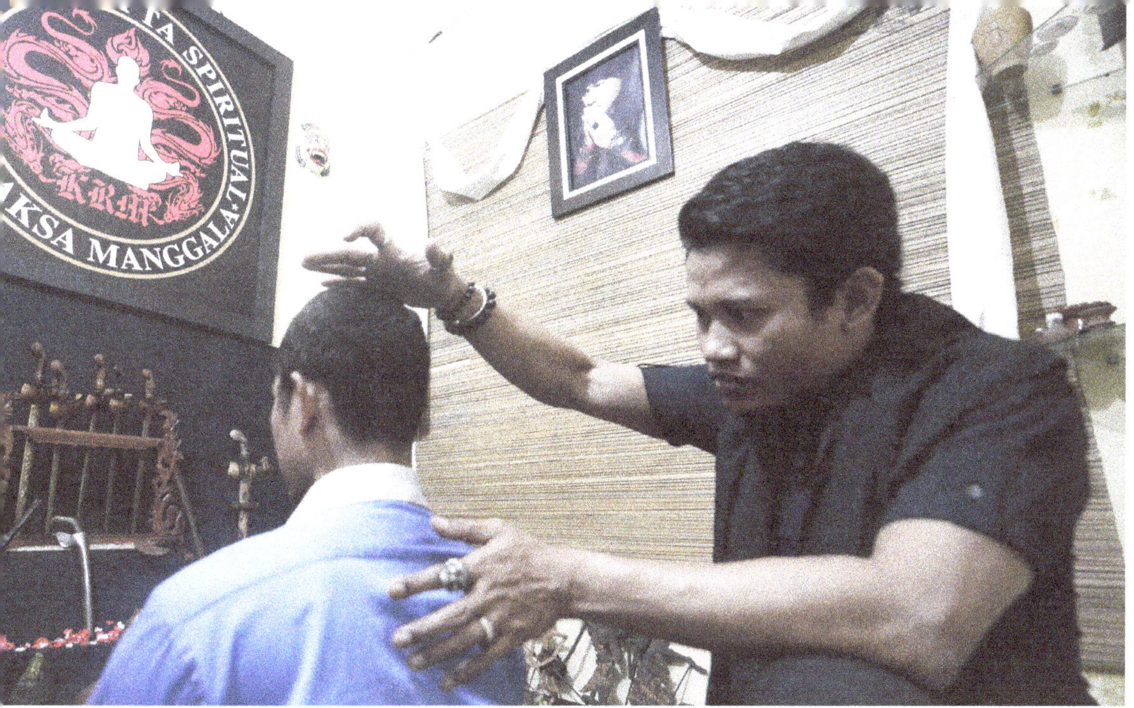

Though Indonesia has the world's largest Muslim population, it is also home to a diverse range of religious groups, including cults and cultlike groups. Pictured is a faith healer at work in Jakarta.

In Indonesia, the transition from the authoritarian Suharto regime to the current democratic system has created an atmosphere of uncertainty and instability. This kind of social instability may influence the emergence of groups that offer instant solutions in the form of personal relationships and eschatological promises, eliminating or at least reducing the feelings of uncertainty.

Some people may be attracted to these groups as they consider established religions have failed. They may feel these religions are focused on the past and can no longer provide guidance in solving social problems. Additionally, they may feel established religions have rigid, unattractive and scary rules.

New religious movements usually evolve in a certain pattern. They start by offering to refresh people's understanding of religious teachings. This is followed by suggestions of a new way of seeing the established religion. Then they justify the possibility of a different view from the established religion. In the end, followers are encouraged to separate from the parent religion.

Almost all new religious movements undergo this metamorphosis. Some manage to become new established religions, like Bahá'ism, but

Fast Fact

According to the Pew Research Center, sixty-four nations have high or very high restrictions on religion. That's about one third of the world's countries, and some of those countries have very large populations. That means nearly 70 percent of the world's population lives in countries with high restrictions on religion.

often the movements disappear with the death of a leader, internal conflict, or because it was banned by a regime.

Dealing With New Religious Movements

There are many types of new religious movements. Some are pacifists, focused on mobilising followers in a peaceful way. Some are extremists.

The US Branch Davidian sect led by David Koresh in Waco, Texas, or the Aum Shinrikyo sect led by Shoko Asahara in Japan shows how these movements can resort to extreme actions when they cannot find a compromise with established religion or authorities.

The Branch Davidians chose armed conflict with the police. Aum Shinrikyo released sarin poison in Tokyo's subway.

These cults are able to mobilise people to carry out extreme actions due to followers' obedience to the leader. This is one of the concerns about the emergence of a new religious movement: the potential harm, as a consequence of blind faith in charismatic leaders, that might result from these movements.

Nevertheless, the Indonesian government should guarantee religious freedom to anyone, including members of religious minorities. Perpetrators of violence, including those who attacked the Gafatar camp, should be brought to justice.

Government officials and law enforcement officers who allowed violence to happen by merely standing by, or who were actively involved in attacks, should be punished.

Indonesia's law allows the government to control religious life in the public sphere. The government can limit certain freedoms in public matters if necessary. But it should do so in line with public interests and fairness.

In dealing with new religious movements, the government should investigate whether a movement has the potential to jeopardise public order before taking action against it.

The government should ban an organisation that preaches violence, allows child marriages or incest, declares a separatist intention, or aims to change the country's constitution into a religious-based one.

Most of the time, attackers of unorthodox religious sects get away with carrying out violence. Meanwhile, groups such as Gafatar end up being confronted with an iron fist. The government often bans religious sects without strong evidence that they are violating public order.

Oppressive measures are not effective in controlling the emergence of new religious movements. Banning groups would make them martyrs. In the end, this would only trigger new religious movements in different models and forms.

EVALUATING THE AUTHOR'S ARGUMENTS:

In this viewpoint, the author argues that governments should only ban religious groups in a few extreme circumstances. Do you agree? Should governments protect all religious groups and only prosecute specific crimes? Should they take action against any new religious movement that may hurt people? Why or why not?

Chapter 3

What Should We Do About Cults and Sects?

Some state and national legislators have passed laws limiting the rights of cults and sects, while others have created laws to protect them.

Viewpoint 1

When Protecting Religion Harms Children

"Idaho legislators ... are shielding what amounts to a religious cult — a cult that endangers its youngest and most vulnerable members."

Leah Sottile

In the following viewpoint, the author reports on a pattern of child deaths in Idaho. The parents followed a Christian sect that did not believe in modern medicine. In Idaho, parents are not breaking the law when they pray for their children instead of seeking medical help. Yet in many states, they can be held legally responsible for the death of a child who was denied medical intervention. This is because in Idaho, laws protecting religious freedom also protect faith healing. This means children can die of treatable diseases because they were denied medical care, and their parents cannot be prosecuted for it. Some people in Idaho want to change the laws, but others are afraid that lessening protections for faith healers would lead to fewer protections for religious groups in general. The author explores perspectives from both sides of the issue. Leah Sottile is a freelance journalist who has written for *High Country News*, which covers issues and stories about the American West.

AS YOU READ, CONSIDER THE FOLLOWING QUESTIONS:

1. Why are some Idaho lawmakers afraid to change laws that protect faith healers?
2. Why do other people believe that faith healers should not have the legal protection in question?
3. How many states have laws protecting faith healers?

In March 2011, the county coroner arrived at a Caldwell, Idaho home, to find a pale 22-month-old boy dead in his mother's arms. The child had been teething, his parents said, when they noticed a rattling cough in his chest. They didn't take him to a doctor. Instead, they told the coroner, they prayed over him.

The family belongs to the Followers of Christ, a Christian sect, concentrated in Idaho, that doesn't believe in modern medicine. When they get sick, even when they're dying, the Followers of Christ avoid doctors and rely solely on prayer.

Six days after the baby's death, the same coroner was called to a different home across town. There, she found a 14-year-old boy in a brown cotton sleeper—who'd also had a rattling behind his ribs dead on his mother's lap. "There were no signs of trauma," the coroner wrote.

A 2013 report by the Idaho Child Fatality Review team noted that since state agencies don't compile the necessary data, "it is difficult to estimate the actual number of preventable deaths to children of religious objectors." But at least 20 times in the past 10 years, southern Idaho coroners have examined the dead children of Followers of Christ members. They died from treatable ailments: Babies had fevers, teenagers had food poisoning, newly born infants gasped for air for hours until their bodies gave up. Or they were stillborn—carried to full-term by mothers who never sought prenatal care.

It's not illegal to believe in faith healing, to *believe* that God will heal his loyal believers. But in many states, parents who choose prayer over medicine can be charged with negligent homicide if their child dies.

Not in Idaho.

For the past few years, a fierce debate over religious freedom has raged in Idaho's Capitol. On one side are lawmakers who fear that

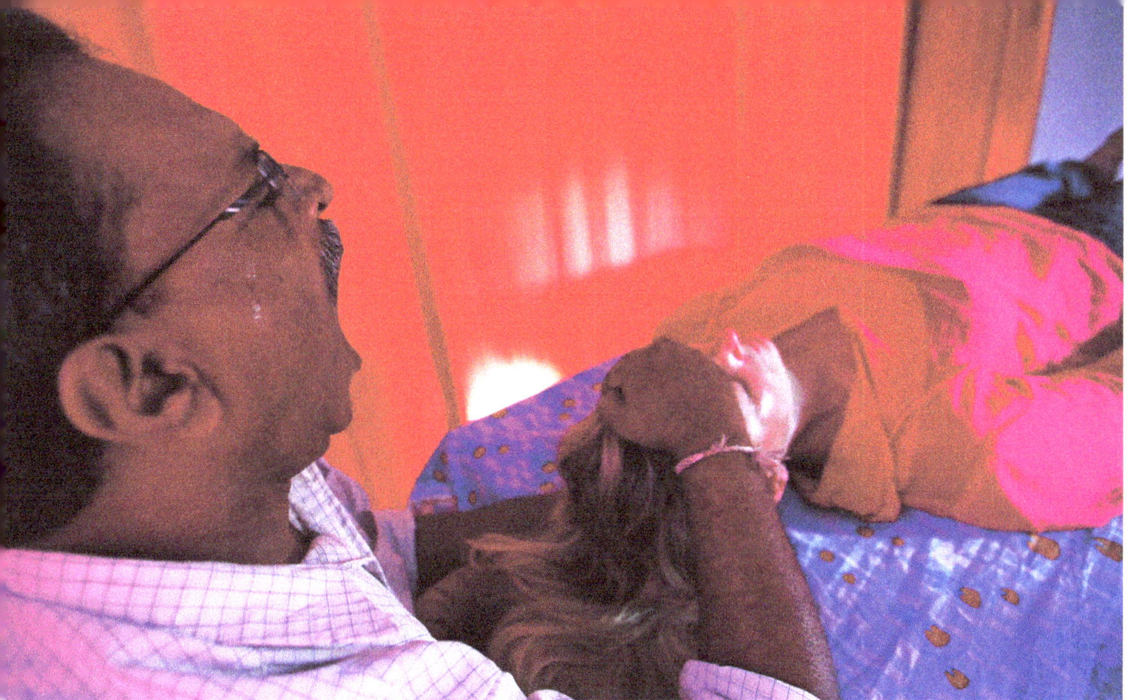

Faith healers can be found in countries around the world, including the United States. The faith healer pictured above is in Kerala, South India.

rolling back protections for faith healers could ultimately infringe on other religious freedoms, and parents who believe that no government entity should tell them how to raise their children. On the other are children's health advocates and ex-Followers of Christ who worry that more children will die if something isn't done—and done fast.

All this is happening at the confluence of several heated national conversations, involving states' rights, identity politics and religious freedom, one that's playing out now in the state with life-or-death consequences.

Idaho, long a beacon for conservatism and libertarianism, has the strongest protections for faith-healers in the West. It is one of just six states nationwide that shield faith-healing parents from felony charges—negligent homicide, manslaughter or capital murder—when their children die of treatable illnesses.

Even as other states, including neighboring Oregon, have rolled back similar protections for faith healers, Idaho has, in some ways, dug in its heels. Last year, in considering a 2017 bill to modify the law, Sen. Lee Heider, R-Twin Falls, said Idaho shouldn't be "in the practice of taking away the constitutional rights of a small few in the name of goodness, correctness, medical appropriateness."

Laws protecting faith healing initially passed in the early 1970s. It took decades for lawmakers to revisit the issue, but so far, no proposed changes have passed.

In October 2013, a 5-day-old baby boy born to Followers of Christ died of a bowel blockage in a Caldwell home. The child's father told the coroner there that the parents did not seek medical treatment despite the fact that "the baby had not had a bowel movement" and had a scrotum swollen to four times the normal size.

Months later, in early 2014, Rep. John Gannon, D-Boise, sought to allow the prosecution of parents who rely on faith-healing "whenever a child's medical condition may cause death or permanent disability." But Gannon's efforts went nowhere. The *Idaho Press-Tribune* reported that Idaho lawmakers said "there's no room in this Legislature for debate on the measure."

Later that year, a baby girl named Fern, in Canyon County, was stillborn. The coroner noted, "It was apparent that she had been dead for a while as the skin was slipping off the entire torso of the body." Not all stillbirths are preventable, but according to a nonprofit called Children's Healthcare is a Legal Duty, which advocates for more stringent laws, there is some evidence that stillbirths are higher among the Followers of Christ. In one Idaho cemetery owned by the sect, 35 percent of the graves from 2002 to 2013 are for minors or stillborn babies.

In 2015, instead of rolling back protections, Idaho legislators reinforced them, passing a "parental rights" bill that ensured parents "have a fundamental right to make decisions concerning the care, custody, education and control of their children."

A month later, a full-term baby girl was stillborn in a Payette home. The next year, the governor called for a task force to examine the issue.

Finally, the bill put forward in 2017 failed, and the cycle continued: Lawmakers dismiss attempts to protect children in faith-healing communities, children continue to die.

Months after Heider and 23 other legislators voted down the bill, a 3-year-old boy died in Parma, Idaho.

When the coroner arrived at the remote trailer, the mother said the boy had seizures. He'd thrown up while he was napping, she said, and she couldn't wake him up again.

Linda Martin has binders filled with coroners' reports from Idaho dating back decades. An ex-Follower of Christ who left the church as a teenager, Martin has been one of the most determined opponents of Idaho's legal tolerance of faith-healing. And she fears that with a right-wing president in the White House, lawmakers will continue to do nothing.

Last spring, President Donald Trump signed an executive order aimed at strengthening protection for religious people in America. "We will not allow people of faith to be targeted, bullied or silenced anymore," he said from the White House rose garden. "In my opinion, when Trump got elected it, it actually empowered the conservative religious Republicans in Idaho," Martin says.

Bruce Wingate, founder of the Protect Idaho Children Foundation, agrees.

Idaho lawmakers "fear that America is under attack, that the religious freedom of America is under attack. They fear gun control is under attack. They fear that every non-conservative point is under attack," he says. "Idaho, they feel, is one of the refuge centers for preventing this and maintaining freedoms."

Attempts to reconsider faith-healing protections, he says, become "ideological questions of 'Do we have freedom of religion or do we not?' "

Critics and legal scholars argue that protecting religious freedom is less important than saving the lives of children. "I think an argument that we don't want to open the floodgates to scrutinizing religions misses the point. No one questions the right of faith healers to *believe* in faith healing," says Shaakirah Sanders, an associate professor of law at the University of Idaho. But belief and practice are two different things. "This is really about minors — individuals who don't have the capacity to make decisions for themselves."

In the summer of 2016, Daniel Sevy stood at a wooden podium in a red plaid shirt, a kerchief tied around his neck. As a member of the Followers of Christ, a notoriously secretive institution, he was invited by lawmakers to speak about his beliefs to the Children at Risk Faith Healing working group. (Sevy declined *High Country News*' multiple requests for an interview after discussions with other church leaders: "We wish our view could be covered in a better manner than

Fast Fact

Followers of Christ Church reside mainly in Idaho, Oregon, and Oklahoma. They practice faith healing, which uses prayers and gestures in attempts to heal physical or mental diseases. Other churches may use a similar name but are not associated with this group.

has been done so far," he wrote, "But we lack confidence in all forms of media at this time.")

"This is a way of life. We live it day to day, every day. If we are injured, sometimes we just pick up and go on," he told the group. And if it's more serious? "We refer to the Lord to take care of us."

In emails obtained by *High Country News* between Sevy and Sen. Dan Johnson, R-Lewiston, Sevy was more forceful: "If these people really had children's welfare at heart, they would support the rights of parents to protect children from a runaway medical profession attempting to bring state oppression to anyone opposing their monopoly!"

Three years ago, when a TV reporter knocked on Sevy's front door, he told him, "Whenever you try to restrict on person or another in any fashion, then you're chipping at freedom. Yours and mine."

In some ways, that's in line with the libertarian and conservative religious political culture of Idaho. In an essay titled "The Power and the Glory," Jill Gill, a Boise State University history professor, writes that "faith groups have strongly shaped Idaho's infrastructure, economics, politics, and cultures."

Historically "Idaho has always been seen as a refuge of sorts for religious groups that are not mainstream," she says in an email.

State Sen. Grant Burgoyne, D-Boise, told *High Country News* that he has drafted a bill on faith healing for the next session. And Gannon said in a statement that he'll continue to push for his bill to be considered this year. "I continue to support my bill to require parents to get medical care when a child's condition may result in permanent injury or death."

Faith-healers aren't the bad people they're made out to be, some legislators say. "They are hard-working, dependable people," Sen. Patti Anne Lodge said last year. "They take care of each other and they take care of themselves."

But Linda Martin believes that statements like that miss the point altogether. Idaho legislators, she says, are shielding what amounts to a religious cult—a cult that endangers its youngest and most vulnerable members.

The church is "part of the community. They're hiding in plain sight," she says. "You don't know what's going on behind closed doors unless you're behind that closed door."

And what's happening behind those doors, she says, is deadly.

EVALUATING THE AUTHOR'S ARGUMENTS:

In this viewpoint, some sources quoted believe faith healing should have legal protection. Others think faith healers should be prosecuted if children die without medical treatment. Does the viewpoint author seem to agree with one group or the other? In your opinion, which group makes the best case in the article? Why do you think this?

France Bans Cults to Protect People

Gerry Hadden

"If someone does something wrong, it is not a fact of religions."

In the following viewpoint, the author interviews a woman who helps people struggling with what she considers to be cults. She founded the group when her daughter joined the Jehovah's Witnesses. This group is legal in the United States and is widely considered a Christian sect, but in France it is considered a cult. The French government investigates and prosecutes cults considered a threat to the state, including groups that are accepted in the United States. French law allows longer jail times and higher fines when crimes are committed with the help of psychological manipulation. Some sources quoted claim the French government is rightly protecting vulnerable people. Others feel that the government unfairly harasses religious groups. Gerry Hadden is the Europe correspondent for Public Radio International's the *World*.

AS YOU READ, CONSIDER THE FOLLOWING QUESTIONS:

1. Why do some people feel cults should be investigated and controlled?
2. What led to the French law against cults?
3. What was this law trying to accomplish?

"The French want to make society safe for religion by banning so-called cults," by Gerry Hadden, Public Radio International, July 12, 2014. Reprinted by permission.

One fall day, way back in 1986, Charline Delporte lost her daughter—to a cult.

"Her new friends just showed up and they packed her things into a van," Delporte remembers. "She said to us, 'OK, well, I'm out of here. Good luck to you both.' I was crying like a baby. I said, 'Blandine, think for a moment, this isn't you. You don't behave like this.'"

"'Whatever,' she said. 'Goodbye.' 'Where you going?' I asked. But she wouldn't say."

This followed months of erratic behavior in which Delporte's bright, inquisitive daughter dropped out of school, often locking herself in her room to pray for hours on end.

Blandine, then 20, went to Paris. She began a new life going door-to-door, preaching the word of her new faith. Charline says she didn't hear from her daughter for years until a postcard came in the mail announcing her wedding. Charline went. When she saw her daughter in her wedding dress, she broke down.

"I was devastated," she says. "I couldn't stay for the whole wedding. My husband had to take me out because I was so upset. On one side of the aisle was our family; on the other, 150 Jehovah's Witnesses."

That's right: Jehovah's Witnesses. In the US, it's a perfectly legal denomination. But in France, it's considered a cult.

France is perhaps Europe's most secular country. For more than a century, separation of church and state has been enshrined in federal law. To defend this principle, the French government is willing to endure controversies like protests over its ban on religious wear in school: no Christian crucifixes and no Muslim veils.

But in one corner of spiritual life, the French state does more than maintain the secular dress code: it actively investigates and prosecutes groups it considers a threat to the state as cults. That includes Jehovah's Witnesses, Scientologists and many forms of Pentacostal Protestantism that are also perfectly acceptable in the US. Some 300 groups are listed by the French state as displaying "cult-like tendencies," such as manipulating people who are mentally weak, separating members from their biological families or demanding too much money, just to name a few.

For help, Charline turned to a tiny, two-room office in the northern city of Lille. It's a place where people struggling with cults can come for help.

There are over eight million Jehovah's Witnesses around the world. Distributing literature, like the Jehovah's Witnesses pictured above, is a well-known characteristic of the group. Despite the group's sizable membership, they are denied legal protections in some countries.

Charline arrived 25 years ago and never left. Today, she runs this government-funded help center, called ADFI. It's one of around 50 such offices across France.

Charline says she receives about five new visitors a week. On a recent morning, she saw a "recovering Jehovah's Witness," a woman whose sister ran off with a group of crystal-healers and a man bilked of his money by a network of phony shrinks.

All of these people were walk-ins, but this ADFI office doesn't just wait around for people to find them. Delporte says she also runs an informal network of spies.

"We have here some young, well-balanced guys whom we can call upon. We call them our 007s," she explains. "We sent them out to listen in at suspicious talks. They'll even pay the entrance fee. It's perfectly normal. The idea is just to see what the group in question is up to so that we can help people."

Spend any time with Charline and one thing becomes clear: she believes she's on a mission. But the groups she's after, the ones on the government cult list, have a different view. They complain that these taxpayer-funded centers constitute an unfair attack on freedom of expression.

Eric Roux, the president of the Union of the Churches of Scientology in France, is a thin man in a sharp suit. He works out of Scientology's headquarters in downtown Paris, a modern, all-white building with a reading room and a lobby filled with books by Scientology's founder, L. Ron Hubbard.

Roux says the state's definition of cult behavior is so fuzzy that it's nearly impossible for religious groups to defend against accusations of wrong-doing.

"If you start to say people are being manipulated because they believe in something which is not true, then you will have a problem with every religion," Roux argues. "Your belief is yours. Even if I convince you to be a Scientologist, for example, that is your right. It doesn't mean that you have been mentally manipulated."

Roux says the government's blacklist of cult-like groups is arbitrary and often contains groups respected in other countries. A couple of decades ago, he says, the Baptists were on it.

"If you were on this list, you were to be prosecuted and targeted," he says, meaning that groups become the subjects of endless investigation and harrassment. Roux calls it hysteria with the force of law, and it's been going on since 1995.

That was the year members of a group called the Order of the Solar Temple staged collective suicides in Canada, Switzerland and France. It shocked the French. The National Assembly soon drew up its first list of suspicious groups and passed a law to go after them specifically.

"Until the law was passed, if someone was raped, there was a normal procedure. The benefit of the law is that if the rape is carried out by means of mental manipulation, then there is an extra punishment," says Catherine Picard, a former deputy in the National Assembly who co-sponsored the legislation. The law allows for longer jail times or steeper fines.

The same goes for financial manipulation, like tricking a wealthy old lady into signing over her fortune. Picard says the law actually protects freedom of religious expression by keeping people free from charlatans.

Fast Fact

The United States protects freedom of religion in the First Amendment to the US Constitution. However, any group can be prosecuted for illegal behavior such as kidnapping or statutory rape.

"The state oversees spiritual groups by auditing them, but we don't control doctrine," she explains. "The state lets anyone choose to join any religion or not join. You're free to believe in aliens or in churches that aren't really churches."

One of those not-really-churches, the French govenrnment believes, is based inside an elaborate mountaintop temple in France's southwest. It's named Mandarom Village and is the birthplace of one of France's oldest and most controversial spiritual groups: The Aumists.

"The name is Mondarom, that means mountain of Om," says Christine Mori, an Aumist nun. "[W]e are for unity of all religions. We are called Aumisme, because it is derived from Om, a sound that many people repeat: Buddhism; and for Christians, it is amen; for Muslims, ameen."

Mori says the government's claim that people can worship as they please is false. She says authorities have been harrassing them since the Aumists' founding guru was accused of rape 20 years ago. Whatever he may have done, Mori says, using the law to go after an entire movement is unfair.

"It is not the group, it is the person," she argues. "If someone does something wrong, it is not a fact of religions."

The Mandarom guru, who claimed he was the son of God, is long gone—he died before his case went to trial. But his voice lives on, echoing from speakers off the 50-foot statues of Krishna, the Buddha, Christ and other deities that rise from the remote mountaintop.

The police have raided the temple many times over the years, even blowing up one of the statues. But Mori says she feels optimistic that the French state will finally recognize Mandarom as a legitimate religion—because Europe already has.

Last year, the European Court for Human Rights ordered France to pay back millions of euros in taxes levied on donations to the Aumists. The ruling, in effect, recognized them as a tax-exempt religious institution.

"We have won, and now they have to consider that we are a religion," Mori says. "But, you know, sometimes the authorities decide something, but after the people? To change the mentality, it takes time. So we have to change the mentality now. But we have time."

The French government is infuriated by the ruling, and it says the fight is not finished: neither against the Aumists nor other cults. It currently has 400 cases before the courts under the anti-cult law.

Charline Delporte says the state *should* continue to go after criminal groups. But she also hopes for more support for her work on the front lines, helping the desperate people who walk through her door every day trying to leave cults.

"'I have no more family, they tell me. Or, 'my kids won't talk to me. I did terrifying things. How can I regain my dignity?'" she says. "It's the person in front of me that matters."

EVALUATING THE AUTHOR'S ARGUMENTS:

In this viewpoint, some sources argue that people have the right to any belief they choose. Does the government have the right or responsibility to interfere with people's beliefs if they have the potential to cause harm? Why or why not? If they do have the right to interfere, under what circumstances is this acceptable? How did this viewpoint influence your opinion?

Viewpoint 3

We Need to Know the Truth About Cults

"Bad news tends to be good news for the media: 'Heartbroken mother loses child to evil cult' is a more compelling headline than 'Young man converts to new religion.' "

Eileen Barker

In the following viewpoint, the author notes that new religious movements (NRMs) are often greeted with suspicion. For thousands of years, people have been punished for turning to new religions. This pattern continues even today: in recent decades, several anti-cult groups have been established. There are a number of good reasons for wanting to learn more information about NRMs. For instance, someone may be deciding whether to join a group. She may want to understand what a family member or client believes. She may want to know whether the group is dangerous, either as a terrorist organization or to its members. Reporters may need information to help them cover a story involving a NRM. However, the author says, the information most people uncover often isn't accurate. People tend to only hear the negatives. Eileen Barker is a sociologist of religion who has been researching minority religions since the early 1970s. She founded the Information Network Focus on Religious Movements (Inform).

"What should we do about the cults?" by Eileen Barker, London School of Economics. Reprinted by permission.

AS YOU READ, CONSIDER THE FOLLOWING QUESTIONS:

1. Why does the author argue it can be helpful for people to have accurate information about the practices of an NRM?
2. What are some of the stances different countries take toward NRMs?
3. Why do most people mainly hear the negative stories about NRMs?

History is full of instances in which citizens with a vested interest in preserving the status quo have greeted anything new with suspicion and distrust. This is certainly true so far as new religious movements (NRMs) are concerned. Once alternatives to traditional beliefs and practices emerge, it is not long before the cry goes up insisting that something ought to be done about the 'cult' or 'sect' that is threatening not only innocent individuals but also the very fabric of society. The Old Testament is full of instances testifying to this; the early Christians were thrown to the lions; the Cathars were burned at the stake; the early days of Islam were hardly conducive to friendly interfaith dialogue; there were the splits between the Eastern Orthodox Churches and the Church of Rome; then there was the Reformation, followed by numerous schisms within the Protestant tradition. Early Protestant "cult-watching groups" (CWGs) attacked both the "whore of Babylon" (Hislop, 1916) and heresies such as the Amish, Doukabours, Anabaptists and Methodists.

[...]

The present wave of new religions in the West started to become visible to the general public towards the end of the 1960s, although several had been around for at least a decade (some much longer). By the 1970s, and particularly after the Jonestown tragedy in 1978, there was an increasing number of demands made to local, national or international authorities to do something about the movements. Among the most vociferous voices to be heard were those of a number of CWGs, some of which began to take matters into their own hands, illegally kidnapping members of NRMs in order to forcibly "deprogramme" them.

Hostility and suspicion toward those with other religions is a problem for many religious groups, mainstream or new. Sometimes police and law enforcement must intervene to protect religious groups. Pictured above are police guarding a mosque afer the 2019 mass shootings at two mosques in Christchurch, New Zealand.

[...]

What Should Be Done?

Opinions about what exactly needs to be done about NRMs vary according to time, place and individuals. For some, the movements and their members should be obliterated altogether; they should be outlawed or "liquidated" (which frequently results in the members going underground, risking imprisonment or even death). A second position is that NRMs should be subject to special laws that restrict their practices (not allowing them to become legal entities so they are unable to assemble for religious ceremonies; forbidding their participation in certain jobs or political parties; or denying them the right to proselytise by speaking of their beliefs or distributing their literature).

Yet another position (generally held by the governments of North America, Britain, the Netherlands and Scandinavian countries—and Inform) is that members of new religions should be treated in just the same way as all other citizens in a democratic country. If the movements or their members break the law they should be tried and punished like any other criminal. If they live within the law, they should not be subjected to special treatment because of their beliefs any more than Methodists or Catholics in contemporary Western society are subject to special regulation purely because of their beliefs. When the Manson Family or Aum Shinrikyo murdered innocent members of the public, it was because of the murders, not because of Manson's or Asahara's religious beliefs, that the law needed to be brought to bear. Those of this opinion accept that new laws or regulations might have to be introduced because of some hitherto unregulated practices undertaken by the NRMs, but this is with the proviso that the new law would apply equally to all citizens, be they members of a new religion, an old religion or no religion. They will also agree that, while not actually falling foul of the law, various groups, including NRMs, indulge in anti-social behaviour. They may, consequently, be of the opinion that the general public should have access to reliable information about the movements not only so that allegedly criminal behaviour can be investigated, but also so that individuals and other groups can reach their own decisions as to how they want to respond to the movements—whether, for example, they would like to join a particular movement, or to engage in interfaith dialogue with it or to rent it a room. Such information could either alert or reassure, depending on different movements, different aspects of a particular movement, and on the values and opinions of those obtaining the information. A mother might, for example, be worried to learn that the NRM her daughter has joined follows a strict vegetarian diet, but is reassured to learn that it promotes celibacy. The girl's father might be unconcerned about the diet, but, hoping to have a grandchild, be upset about the practice of celibacy. Another parent is anxious that her son will not achieve eternal salvation as he has rejected the Christian faith in which he was raised, yet she could be highly relieved that he has stopped taking dangerous drugs.

It is not only relatives who want to gain information about NRMs. There are religious or spiritual seekers, eager to find a movement that will answer questions for which they have been unable to obtain answers from traditional religions. There are evangelical Christians wanting to know about theological deviations. There

Fast Fact

Aum Shinrikyo is a Japanese doomsday cult that was founded in 1984. It is known for carrying out a deadly sarin attack on a Tokyo subway in 1995.

are social workers, clergy, medical practitioners, counsellors, therapists, lawyers and/or teachers, whose clients, parishioners, patients or students are (or could become) associated with an NRM. Police and lawyers will be concerned about criminal or deviant behaviour; those responsible for national security will want to know about a movement's capacity to carry out terrorist attacks; those responsible for social security issues and mental health practitioners may want to know about hygiene, diet, child labour and various other practices. These and further questions will also be of interest to reporters, writers, scholars, human rights activists and various others who will themselves become suppliers of information to a wider public. And there are persons involved in policy decisions, either as legislators or as administrators or law-enforcement agents charged with the practical application of the law, who are also eager to obtain information about the movements.

While most of these people will claim that they want to hear the truth about the NRM(s) in which they are interested, several are in fact looking for an evaluative judgement. Some may want to be reassured that a particular religion is "good"; others may want to hear that NRMs are all evil or that they have some sort of supernatural powers that force people to join them. Some may want to hear that a charismatic leader has received revelations from God—others that s/he is a fraudulent confidence trickster who disseminates false prophecy. And there is no doubt that people who are looking for such judgements can find amongst the cult-watching groups those that specialise in the provision of negative information and others, including the movements themselves, which produce only positive images.

The vast majority of people who acquire information about NRMs are, however, unlikely to have been actively shopping for any information at all. Their knowledge of the movements will have been gained almost by accident, in a haphazard fashion, through reports in the mass media, or possibly second or third-hand accounts through their personal networks, or, occasionally, a chance encounter with a proselytising member in a public place. Numerous studies indicate, firstly, that the most influential sources of information about NRMs are the media, and, secondly, that the majority of that information is of a negative nature. This is not surprising when one considers that the media have an interest in attracting and keeping readers, viewers, and listeners, most of whom are likely to be attracted by novel, 'sexy', sensational or horror stories. Bad news tends to be good news for the media: *Heartbroken mother loses child to evil cult* is a more compelling headline than *Young man converts to new religion.* Since the media have expanded to include the Internet, where accountability is almost entirely absent, an ever-increasing supply of fallacious rubbish is to be found.

It is difficult to assess precisely how much influence the media have on "inadvertent consumers," but there is little doubt that it is considerable and that this can result in widespread support for demands by more active participants to 'do something about the cults'.

[...]

The basic aim of Inform, to help enquirers by providing reliable, up-to-date information, requires the collection, assessment and dissemination of a considerable quantity of material. Inform's collection of data comes from all available sources, including the movements themselves, their opponents, former members, families of members, the media and an international network of experts and specialists, which includes scholars, professionals such as lawyers, doctors, counsellors, clergy, other CWGs—and anyone else who might be able to help. The openness with which we receive information does not, of course, mean that it is all considered reliable or given equal weight. Assessment is a crucial part of the exercise in that it is on this that Inform bases its claim that the information it disseminates is as accurate and balanced as possible.

[...]

EVALUATING THE AUTHOR'S ARGUMENTS:

In this viewpoint, the author argues that most people only hear negative information about NRMs. Do you think this is true? When considering NRMs and cults, is it important to keep in mind all perspectives on these groups? Do all perspectives deserve equal consideration?

Helping People Leave Cults Is a Delicate Operation

"The families and friends of cult members often suffer in relative silence for years"

Rick Ross

In the following excerpted viewpoint, a cult expert offers advice on how to respond when a loved one joins a cult. He advises people to educate themselves about cults before trying to intervene. Family and friends should avoid criticizing or offending the cult member. Instead, they should maintain a friendly connection. Confrontation might lead to the cult member cutting off family and friends altogether. The author says there's no easy way to get someone out of a cult. Instead, the goal is to maintain connections until the cult member is ready to leave. Rick Ross is a cult specialist and founder of the nonprofit Cult Education Institute.

AS YOU READ, CONSIDER THE FOLLOWING QUESTIONS:

1. Why does the author advise people to remain calm and avoid hasty action?
2. Why should people researching cults be suspicious about the information they find?
3. Why should people avoid acting hostile to someone who joins a cult?

"Coping With Cult Members," by Rick Ross, Cult Education Institute, October 2000. Reprinted by permission.

[...]

When someone you know becomes involved in a destructive cult there is one rule, which is consistently applicable to any cult situation—don't act hastily or panic. It is unwise to offer any response without first educating yourself—by specifically researching the group/leader in question, the general subject of cults and carefully considering what response best suits your individual situation. After this process of education you will better understand your options and can develop a practical strategy.

Remember once you respond—you may have to live with the results of that response for some time.

In any contact with a cult member it is vitally important to remain (at least visibly) calm. It is also important, whenever possible, to discuss the situation with other family members and/or those intimately concerned. Any strategy or planned response is best approached when everyone concerned is acting together in concert and fully informed. It may also be helpful to seek a second opinion from someone objective who is not personally involved, but ideally is knowledgeable about cults—such as a family therapist/counselor, clergy person or specialist regarding cults.

[...]

Communication

Whenever family and friends are concerned about someone in a cult—communication with the cult member is vitally important and should be ongoing. Hopefully, the group and its leaders will allow that communication and not interfere with any existing relationships. Most often when family and friends are not visibly hostile and remain at least seemingly passive—communication will be allowed.

Communication is absolutely essential for the following two primary reasons:

Heaven's Gate was a cult founded by Marshall Applewhite (pictured*) and Bonnie Nettles in the United States in 1974. They led a mass suicide of thirty-nine of the group's members in 1997.*

- First, to demonstrate continuing love and commitment, which should remain intact regardless of cult involvement.
- Second, because by communicating you can offer the cult member a link to the outside world, more accurate feedback and an outside frame of reference.

Communication thus often enables you to effectively penetrate the cult's control over a member's environment and his or her information. And also most importantly their thoughts and emotional life. Whenever you talk to a cult member you should always try to stay positive. Find subjects of mutual interest and attempt to maintain and/or build upon your rapport. Be friendly, reasonable and look for areas of possible agreement. Don't be confrontational, punitive, combative and/or argumentative. Don't denounce the group, its leader(s) and/or beliefs and practices. But this does not mean that you should be deliberately misleading or phony. Don't give false information and/or act obviously out of character. Never use the word "cult" to describe the group or terms like "brainwashed" and "mind control."

If a cult member confronts you with their beliefs and demands a response, defer such an exchange by simply saying—"I have my own beliefs, but I would be willing to look at some literature, books or materials from your perspective." If they are persistent and confrontational you might say, "I would rather not discuss this now—let's talk about something else. I don't want to argue." And "I am just so glad to have this time with you—let's make our time together pleasant."

Frequent contact is very important if at all possible. This may include phone calls, letters and/or personal visits, but don't be a pest. That is, reasonably respect that person's space and schedule. You should probably coordinate any communication efforts with other family members and perhaps the cult member's old friends—encouraging them to visit and call regularly too.

[...]

Conversation

Whenever talking with a cult member it is often meaningful to ask open ended and thought provoking questions, but always without being accusatory or argumentative. For example, ask questions about the future such as, "What are your plans for the next few years?" "Where do you see yourself in five years—what will you be doing then?" Such questions may spark some spontaneous consideration and/or critical thinking. The cult member might consider their role in the group, sense of security, doubts and the future. You might talk about education plans, medical care or even retirement. But again, you must be sensitive to their "loaded language" and the unreasonable fears they may have (e.g. group denunciations concerning education or medicine). You must limit any conversation and comments within such parameters.

When unreasonable fears come up try to put them into a more objective frame of reference by giving accurate feedback such as, "Do you really think that's a serious concern?" And "Why?" Always allow the cult member to answer completely and listen courteously. Be a good listener and don't interrupt or in any way belittle or ridicule their responses.

Again, remember that you may be dealing largely with a cult personality. Be aware that what you think and/or feel is reasonable, rational and logical may not be considered so in the cult.

Ask general questions about their daily life such as—"What did you do this week?" And just simple questions like "How are things going?" It is meaningful to demonstrate some genuine interest in the group, its daily life and activities. Don't ask pointed questions that sound accusatory and again—never use the word "cult" in any conversation.

Encourage family members and old friends to also have conversations with the cult member too. Be sure everyone is aware of the limitations and guidelines for that communication as previously outlined.

Generally, the more communication there is with people outside of the group—the better.

In any conversation with a cult member it is crucial to connect in some way with their past—specifically, before their involvement with the group. In this way you can, in a non-threatening way, often stimulate their submerged and genuine personality. You can do this by recalling memories of happy times spent with family and friends, accomplishments at school, even old romantic interests—without offending the group's sensibilities and/or breaking their rules (e.g. celibacy, banned holidays, prohibited activities). Working within such a framework is often difficult, but it is important to demonstrate to the cult member through passive conversation that his or her past life did have value, happiness and meaning.

Never be aggressive, punitive or try to induce guilt feelings through conversation—the group may turn this around and use it as an indictment of both you and your intentions. Assume that anything you say to the cult member will be repeated to leaders and/or others in the group and scrutinized. Again, don't provide the group and its leaders with ammunition to discredit you. Always do your best to be truthful, positive and consistent. And make every effort to fulfill any commitments.

Being a good listener will also enable you to gather information about the group, its practices, living conditions and whatever jargon they may use. Take notes whenever possible concerning any conversation (e.g. list key words and phrases they use frequently, note their special rules, practices and/or diet). Many cult groups are so small and obscure that there is little if any information readily available about them. Your notes may prove to be an invaluable future resource.

Only the most extreme groups discourage any expression of emotion or endearment. In most groups there is no prohibition against sincere feelings. With this in mind it's important to include in any conversation words of love and regard. You should say, "I love you" and "It's always good to hear from you" or "I miss you."

Life is often hard in a destructive cult and is very important for members to know they have family and friends on the outside who care. And that these people are there to provide loving support. If a cult member considers leaving the group--this may become a vitally important and pivotal point.

[…]

Leaving

Most cult members will eventually walk away from their respective groups. Sadly, this may take place after years of exploitation and personally destructive involvement. Specifically, they may have experienced psychological, emotional and at times financial and physical damage.

It is vitally important to express your unconditional love. Never say, "I told you so" or act in a punitive way or guilt-inducing manner.

Don't make this your opportunity to attack the group and its members. Instead, remember that even a destructive cult experience may not have been totally negative. The member's time within the group may have resulted in some positive changes and realizations such as increased sensitivity, spirituality or the end of some self-destructive behavior (e.g. illegal drug use, drinking). Avoid sweeping generalizations/statements about the group and/or his or her group experience. Again, be a good listener and always be as positive as possible.

This may again be a time to seek qualified and knowledgeable professional help.

Cult Recovery

There are common problems experienced by most former cult members during their recovery period. It is important to recognize that these problems are commonly shared by a majority of ex-members and not to become alarmed or panic. This may include depression, nightmares, anxiety attacks, excessive shame and/or guilt and seemingly unreasonable fears about the future.

Former cult members may at times feel like they are either back in the group, or wish that they were. Such a sensation may be prompted by something that occurs, which is reminiscent of their group experiences or practices. Some people call this "floating." But this does not necessarily happen to every former cult member.

Former members may also take some time to redevelop their critical thinking skills and initiate independent decision-making. Likewise, their ability to tolerate ambiguity may return slowly. Don't expect some instant overnight transformation. And don't pressure them hoping to speed up the recovery process Typically, the longer a person has been in a destructive cult—the longer they may take to recover. Also, recovery may depend upon their degree of personal involvement and/or the level of destructiveness and control within that particular group.

Members in most destructive cults are taught some form of "learned dependency." They are also frequently persuaded that individual autonomy and/or independent decision making are negative or even "sinful." Be understanding and patient. Remember these two important points at all times:

- Don't be critical of spirituality, idealism and/or greater awareness. The stated goals and ideals of the group may have been laudable—despite its behavior.
- Don't try to convince or convert a former cult member about your personal beliefs. Respect their process of recovery and

Fast Fact

"Deprogramming" refers to practices intended to forcibly change the beliefs of those in cults or who hold other controversial beliefs. It often involves kidnapping and coercion, and though it was popular as a response to NRMs and cults in the 1970s, it is now often viewed as a violation of civil rights.

personal discovery. They will make their own choices in their own time and may require a rest from church, religion, and even awareness groups for awhile.

There are rehabilitation facilities specifically designed to help recovering cult members.

Support

Recovering cult members, not unlike others in some form of recovery, can benefit from support groups. There may be a support group for former cult members in your area. Or, you may find resources through the Internet and/or books on the subject of cults. Support groups can help former members through shared experiences, insights and varied perspectives. Former members are likely to feel less alone through their involvement with a support group. They may also realize that many other people have a similar history and often struggle with related recovery issues and problems. But don't pressure an ex-member to attend a support group—simply offer the information and encourage them.

Just as former members may need support—the families and friends of cult members may also find this helpful. Don't hesitate to find your own support group. For example, there are often specific groups for the parents of cult members. Dealing with a cult situation can be exhausting and emotionally draining—a support group may help you to cope more easily with your circumstances and make you feel less isolated.

[…]

The families and friends of cult members often suffer in relative silence for years—waiting for a loved love to leave a destructive group is a painful process based upon love, patience and most of all hope.

EVALUATING THE AUTHOR'S ARGUMENTS:

In this viewpoint, the author says it can take years for someone to leave a cult. Nonetheless, he advises people to avoid confronting family members or friends who are in cults. Are you convinced by his arguments? Why or why not? Are these actions intended to convince a loved one to leave a cult or to provide them a support system? Are we responsible for discouraging loved ones from partaking in damaging behavior?

What to Do When a Loved One Joins a Cult

"It is very hard and sometimes humiliating for cult members to admit to the outside world that they were wrong."

Rod Dubrow-Marshall and Linda Dubrow-Marshall

In the following viewpoint, the authors try to explain why cults can be so appealing and difficult to leave. They suggest ways of talking to someone who has joined a cult and recommend being positive about the person's experience in the cult. This can actually help the cult member recognize where their reality is not matching up with what they wanted. By keeping a positive connection and supporting the cult member, they will be able to turn to you when they want help. Although joining a cult is not necessarily a common experience, the reasons people join them are generally relatable to most people. Rod Dubrow-Marshall is a professor of social psychology. Linda Dubrow-Marshall is a lecturer in applied psychology. They both teach at the University of Salford in Manchester, England.

"How to talk someone out of a damaging cult," by Rod Dubrow-Marshall and Linda Dubrow-Marshall, The Conversation, December 2, 2016. https://theconversation.com/how-to-talk-someone-out-of-a-damaging-cult-68930.

AS YOU READ, CONSIDER THE FOLLOWING QUESTIONS:

1. How can joining a cult be like falling in love, according to the authors?
2. Why do the authors recommend unconditionally loving the cult member?
3. How do the authors suggest supporting someone who decides to leave a cult?

Many of you will know someone who has suddenly fallen head over heels in love with someone. Some will know people who have done likewise—but for a strange religion or group that you've never heard of. What do you say to them? How can you help? And how do you express your concern or surprise at their change of appearance or lifestyle and their utter devotion to someone or something that, to you, seems really crazy?

It's a question we've thought about a lot. We have spent decades talking to current and former members of all kinds of cults, from religious-based groups like the Branch Davidians to political groups on the far right and far left and even psychotherapy cults like the Center For Feeling Therapy. We wanted to understand the attraction of these organisations—and why they're so hard to leave.

The first thing to realise is that people in cults are not crazy but are the same intelligent, creative and interesting individuals they were before. As with falling in love they are just crazy about the group, its amazing leader and its great potential to change the world and them with it. So the ideals of the group are probably quite attractive superficially—ending war and poverty, say, or promoting the healthy development of brain and body. After all, you don't see many adverts saying "join this damaging cult that will destroy your life."

Your friend or loved one has probably fallen hook line and sinker for the positive message of the group and their whole identity is now focused on this message. The key thing to remember is that criticising the group, however strange or damaging it seems to you, is the same as criticising your friend or family member themselves. They love the group really deeply—for all intents and purposes, they *are* the group.

Maintaining an open line of conversation is important when encouraging someone to leave a cult. This involves remaining patient and nonjudgmental when discussing the cult.

Think back to when you fell in love for the first time and got those disapproving looks or critical comments from your parents or friends. Remember how angry that made you feel? And how determined you were to love the person all the more.

The most important piece of advice is to not criticise, condemn or judge, even if you have serious concerns. Instead, focus on why this person identifies with the group so much, and what they believe they are getting from it. And try to reinforce the message: "It's great that you're developing yourself and your skills so positively and that the group is making you so happy."

It may feel cheesy, but the point of this approach is to draw on the psychological technique of motivational interviewing, so that these positive statements, similar to those the person has made themselves, will eventually lead them to question whether they are really true—we call this the "strategic and personal oriented dialogue" approach. This means you have to keep talking. Keep the dialogue going and help your loved one measure the group against their own hopes and standards. In time, the scales will start to fall from their eyes, and you can be ready for that moment.

In truth, damaging cults are often run by charlatans. They offer world peace and the promised land while actually sucking people in, taking over their minds and unduly influencing them to give up their time, money, families and careers without any tangible results. Nirvana is always just around the corner, and cults coerce their members to work ever harder to get to the impossible.

Fast Fact

"Motivational interviewing" is a counseling method that helps clients resolve mixed or contradictory feelings. This can help people find the motivation they need to change their behavior.

Often members are made to feel unworthy and are humiliated. They can never measure up to the ideals and perfection of the leader, and bit by bit their hopes for what the group offers start to crumble. Remind them, supportively, that it's great they're moving forward with their life so positively in the group, and the penny will suddenly drop—"I'm actually not having a good time at all … what on earth am I doing?" Crucially, they will have come to this painful realisation themselves—with your help, but without you forcing it on them.

When what seems like the most loving group of individuals with the best ideas ever turns out to be a really big mistake, it is very hard and sometimes humiliating for cult members to admit to the outside world that they were wrong.

This is where you come in again: be there as the unconditionally loving and caring friend or family member that you really are. Where the cult judges and condemns its members, you will be there as the person who says:

> *Sure, it is a crazy destructive group, but I understand why you got involved. We all fall for con artists and swindlers once in a while—you still have a lot to offer and I can help you move on with your life.*

After the cult, the world can seem a bleak and less exciting place. But, with the help of family and friends, the former member can build a new and more authentic life and purpose. Hang in there and you'll be what they really do need at the end of the rainbow.

EVALUATING THE AUTHORS' ARGUMENTS:

How does the advice presented in this viewpoint compare to the previous author's advice? Which one would you choose to follow, if either? Why? Can the decision to join a cult or NRM be entirely explained and resolved through psychology?

Facts About Cults, Sects, and New Religions

Editor's note: These facts can be used in reports to add credibility when making important points or claims.

Talking About Cults, Sects, and New Religions

- **apostasy:** The abandonment of a religious or political belief. The term may specifically be used to describe a Christian who rejects Christianity.
- **brainwashing:** A method of changing someone's attitudes or beliefs. It can involve the use of force, including methods like torture.
- **church:** A conventional religious organization.
- **cult:** A religious organization that departs from the usual, accepted standards and has novel beliefs and practices.
- **exclusivist:** In religious terms, someone who believes that people will only be saved if they follow a specific religion.
- **heresy:** A belief or opinion that goes against traditional religious beliefs, especially Christian beliefs.
- **inclusivist:** In religious terms, someone who believes that anyone may be saved regardless of the religion they follow.
- **mind control:** Using psychological tactics to manipulate a person's thinking, emotions, or behavior.
- **new religious movements (NRMs):** Contemporary groups identified as either cults or sects, distinguishing them from the traditional religious beliefs of the culture.
- **religion:** The worship of a superhuman, supernatural controlling power. It involves the belief in an unseen power and an unseen world.
- **sect:** A religious organization that has traditional beliefs and practices but departs from the usual, accepted standards.
- **secular:** Attitudes, activities, and other things that do not have a religious or spiritual basis.

Brainwashing and mind control are sometimes used interchangeably. However, some experts separate the techniques. Brainwashing is more likely to involve torture. The victim may see the person attempting to brainwash them as an enemy. However, they may still give in, in order to survive. Prisoners of war may suffer this form of brainwashing.

With mind control, the manipulator is often considered a friend, helper, or mentor. The person being controlled may believe they are making their own decisions. Some people consider marketing and advertising forms of mind control, as they try to manipulate customer behavior. Hypnosis could be considered a form of mind control, but it may be used positively to control a fear or stop a behavior such as smoking. Abusive relationships may involve controlling behavior that could be considered mind control.

Mind control is also called "thought control" or "psychological persuasion."

Recognizing a Cult

Behaviors often associated with cults include:

- Members display unquestioning commitment to the group's leader and his or her beliefs.
- The leaders dictate how members should act, think, and feel. Members may be told what to wear, where to work, and whom to marry.
- Questioning and doubt are discouraged or even punished.
- Leaders use shame and guilt to influence and control members.
- Members may be encouraged or required to cut ties with their family and friends outside the group.
- The group aggressively recruits new members and may hide many aspects of the group at first.

See more "Characteristics Associated with Cultic Groups" from the International Cultic Studies Association at https://www.icsa-home.com/articles/characteristics.

Some people apply the word "cult" to groups that are not religious. Other "cults" may be business organizations, political groups, or self-help or therapy groups. They're most likely to be called cults if they use cult tactics. These often include commitment to a charismatic leader, deceptive recruitment practices, and punishing anyone who disagrees or tries to leave the group.

Statistics Related to Cults, Sects, and New Religions

Because there is no clear, universal definition of a cult, it is impossible to determine the number of cults in the world. Surveys in the late 1990s found an estimated 5,000 cults in the United States. Some are very small, while others may have hundreds of thousands of members. Another researcher estimated 10,000 to 20,000 new religious groups in the world, but only about 1,000 in the United States.

U. Magazine, from Colleges.com, asked readers about cults on campuses. Forty percent of respondents said cults were active on their college campuses. Seventeen percent said they had been members of a cult on campus at some point. Of those people, almost a quarter said they felt pressured into joining. Thirty-five percent thought the group used mind games to control them.

Laws About Cults, Sects, and New Religions

According to a Pew Research Center study published in 2009, sixty-four nations have high or very high restrictions on religion. That's about one third of the world's countries. Some of those have very large populations. That means nearly 70 percent of the world's people live in countries with high restrictions on religion.

Restrictions can be imposed by the government in the form of laws, policies, and actions. They can also result from hostile acts by people and groups.

Among the world's twenty-five most populous countries, Iran, Egypt, Indonesia, Pakistan, and India have the most of these combined restrictions. Brazil, Japan, the United States, Italy, South Africa, and the United Kingdom have the least.

The United States protects freedom of religion under the First Amendment of the Constitution. Cults can legally use "mind control" or pressure people to give all their money to the cult. However, a few cults have been recognized as criminal organizations and are illegal for that reason. In addition, any group can be prosecuted for illegal behavior such as kidnapping or statutory rape.

Organizations to Contact

The editors have compiled the following list of organizations concerned with the issues debated in this book. The descriptions are derived from materials provided by the organizations. All have publications or information available for interested readers. The list was compiled on the date of publication of the present volume; the information provided here may change. Be aware that many organizations take several weeks or longer to respond to inquiries, so allow as much time as possible for the receipt of requested materials.

Berkley Center for Religion, Peace & World Affairs

3307 M St. NW, Suite 200
Washington, DC 20007
phone: (202) 687-5119
email: berkleycenter@georgetown.edu
website: www.berkleycenter.georgetown.edu/
This academic research center at Georgetown University in Washington, DC, is dedicated to the study of religion, ethics, and politics.

Cult Education Institute (CEI)

1977 N. Olden Ave. Ext #272
Trenton, NJ 08618
phone: (609) 396-6684
email: info@culteducation.com
website: www.culteducation.com/
CEI is focused on public education and research. Its stated mission is "to study destructive cults, controversial groups and movements, and to provide a broad range of information and services."

Cult Information and Family Support (CIFS)

PO BOX 3148
North Nowra NSW 2541
Australia

phone: 0423-332-766
email: info@cifs.org.au
website: www.cifs.org.au/
CIFS is an Australian support and information network. It provides support and develops awareness for those affected by cultic relationships.

Cult Information Centre (CIC)

BCM CULTS
London, WC1N 3XX
United Kingdom
phone: 07790 753 035
website: www.cultinformation.org.uk/
CIC is a charity in the United Kingdom. It provides information for victims of cults, their families and friends, researchers, and the media.

Cults: An Undergraduate Library Subject Guide

1402 W. Gregory Drive
Urbana, IL 61801
phone: (217) 333-3477
website: guides.library.illinois.edu/cults
The University of Illinois at Urbana-Champaign provides this library subject guide. Learn about the issues surrounding cults and find books and articles on the subject.

Hartford Institute for Religion Research

77 Sherman Street
Hartford, CT 06105
phone: (860) 509-9542
email: hirr@hartsem.edu
website: hirr.hartsem.edu
This group from the Hartford Seminary conducts rigorous research about what is happening in religious life today. See the section on "New Religious Movements" under the "Denomination"s tab.

The Information Network Focus on Religious Movements (Inform)

c/o Department of Theology and Religious Studies
King's College London
Virginia Woolf Building
22 Kingsway
London WC2B 6LE
United Kingdom
phone: +44 (0)20 7848 1132
email: inform@kcl.ac.uk
website: www.inform.ac
Inform is an organization that aims to offer objective information on religious groups. The group states that they "exist to prevent harm based on misinformation about minority religions and sects by bringing the insights and methods of academic research into the public domain." The website provides leaflets on major religion and on extremism on campus.

International Cultic Studies Association (ICSA)

email: mail@icsamail.com
website: www.icsahome.com
ICSA is a network concerned with psychological manipulation and abuse in cults and other environments. It helps former members, provides guidance to families, and provides study guides and resources.

For Further Reading

Books

Goldberg, Lorna, William Goldberg, Rosanne Henry, and Michael Langone. *Cult Recovery: A Clinician's Guide to Working With Former Members and Families*. Florida: International Cultic Studies Association, 2017. Researchers and clinical workers explore how to help people negatively affected by cult dynamics.

Hassan, Steven. *Combating Cult Mind Control*. Newton, MA: Freedom of Mind Press, 2015. This book includes stories of people in cults. It offers advice on how to avoid mind control and how to help someone in a cult.

Hexham, Irving. *Pocket Dictionary of New Religious Movements: Over 400 Groups, Individuals & Ideas Clearly and Concisely Defined*. Downers Grove, IL: IVP Academic, 2009. The entries in the book cover specific new religious groups and practices.

Jeffs, Rachel. *Breaking Free: How I Escaped Polygamy, the FLDS Cult, and My Father, Warren Jeffs*. New York, NY: Harper, 2017. This memoir tells the story of a girl who grew up in a secretive polygamist cult. The author was forced into marriage and had several children before she escaped.

Singleton, Andrew. *Religion, Culture & Society*. Thousand Oaks, CA: SAGE Publications Ltd, 2014. This book for nonacademic readers explores the social and cultural context of diverse religion. It asks: What is religion? How is religion changing in a modern world? What is the future of religion? These questions are addressed through case studies and observations.

Taylor, Kathleen. *Brainwashing: The science of thought control*. Oxford, UK: Oxford University Press, 2017. Anecdotes and case studies are used in this book to explore the science of "brainwashing."

Tucker, Ruth. *Another Gospel: Cults, Alternative Religions, and the New Age Movement*. Grand Rapids, MI: Zondervan Academic, 2004. This book presents a survey of major alternative religions in the United States. The book explores how alternative religious movements succeed, and related controversies.

Winn, Denise. *The Manipulated Mind: Brainwashing, Conditioning and Indoctrination*. Los Altos, CA: Malor Books, 2017. This book breaks down "brainwashing" into its individual elements. Learn what human characteristics make people more or less susceptible.

Periodicals and Internet Sources

Barber, Nigel, "Faith Healing Shouldn't Work, but It Does," *Psychology Today*, March 2, 2011. https://www.psychologytoday.com/us/blog/the-human-beast/201103/faith-healing-shouldnt-work-it-does

Brown, Fleur, "I grew up in a cult and I can tell you why 'normal' people join them," *Insider*, April 8, 2019. https://www.insider.com/i-grew-up-in-a-cult-and-i-can-tell-you-why-normal-people-join-them-2018-3

DeLashmutt, Gary and Dennis McCallum, " 'Christian' Cults and Sects," Xenos Christian Fellowship. https://www.xenos.org/essays/christian-cults-and-sects

Emont, Jon, "Why Are There No New Major Religions?" *Atlantic*, August 6, 2017. https://www.theatlantic.com/international/archive/2017/08/new-religions/533745/

"Eyewitness: Why people join cults," *BBC News*, March 24, 2000. news.bbc.co.uk/2/hi/africa/688317.stm

Harrison, Guy P., "Why No One Should Ever Use the Word 'Cult'," *Psychology Today*, July 18, 2016. https://www.psychologytoday.com/us/blog/about-thinking/201607/why-no-one-should-ever-use-the-word-cult

Ogloff, James R. P., "Cults and the law: A discussion of the legality of alleged cult activities," *Behavioral Sciences & the Law* 10(1):117-140, December 1992. https://www.researchgate.net/publication/246899268_Cults_and_the_law_A_discussion_of_the_legality_of_alleged_cult_activities

Ross, Rick, "Watch out for tell-tale signs," *Guardian*, May 27, 2009. https://www.theguardian.com/commentisfree/belief/2009/may/27/cults-definition-religion

Schneider, Katy, "The Best Books on Cults, for These Cult-Obsessed Times," *Strategist*, June 1, 2018. http://nymag.com/strategist/article/best-books-on-cults-reviewed-by-experts.html

Stein, Alexandra, "Terror, Love, and Brainwashing," *Psychology Today*, February 2, 2017. https://www.psychologytoday.com/us/blog/the-author-speaks/201702/terror-love-and-brainwashing

Thomas, Michael, "5 Reasons People Join Cults and Cults are Successful," Reachout Trust, January 5, 2017. https://reachouttrust.org/5-reasons-people-join-cults/

Toohill, Kathleen, "Why Do People Join Cults?" June 26, 2017. https://medium.com/s/how-to-cult/why-do-people-join-cults-ecdf-5c6af848

Tormsen, David, "10 Insane Non-Religious Cults," Listverse, April 9, 2015. https://listverse.com/2015/04/09/10-insane-non-religious-cults/

Tyrrell, Ivan, "Exploring the CULT in culture," Human Givens Institute. https://www.hgi.org.uk/resources/delve-our-extensive-library/society-and-culture/exploring-cult-culture

"What is a cult? What is a sect?" CultFAQ.org. http://cultfaq.org/cult-faq-sect-definition.html

"Who Joins Cults, And Why?" Apologetics Index, February 23, 2018. http://www.apologeticsindex.org/265-who-joins-cults-and-why

Websites

Cult Education Institute (CEI) (www.culteducation.com)

CEI studies destructive cults, controversial groups, and movements. The website hosts a large archive of information about controversial groups.

Cult Information Centre (CIC) (www.cultinformation.org.uk)

The CIC website includes links to articles, books, and videos about cults. It also links to helpful organizations in other countries.

Cultwatch (www.cultwatch.com/about.html)
Cultwatch aims to help the people trapped in cults and to warn people about the dangers of cults. Cultwatch is a Christian-based organization.

Understanding World Religions (www.understandingworldreligions.com/)
This site from the University of Calgary offers basic information about the major world religions. You can download a free PDF copy of *The Concise Dictionary of Religion*.

Index

A

apostasy, explanation of, 28
Asahara, Shoko, 70, 89
Aumists, 84–85
Aum Shinrikyo, 70, 89, 90

B

Bainbridge, William Sims, 13, 14, 15
Barker, Eileen, 86–92
Berger, Peter, 16
brainwashing, 8, 18–23, 37, 48, 51, 54, 96
Branch Davidians, 8, 23, 70, 103
Buddhism, 38–43, 84

C

Center for Feeling Therapy, 103
child abuse, and faith healing, 9, 73–79
Christian Assemblies International, 56–60
coercion, as method of indoctrination, 18, 21–23
college campuses, recruitment on, 7, 61–66
community, as step in conversion process, 27
conditioning, as method of indoctrination, 18, 21–23
confirmation bias, 38–43
conversion, as method of indoctrination, 18, 21–23
conversion experience, five steps of, 25–28
Coxon, Kate, 61–66
crime, and cults, 67–71, 84
cults, overview of types of, 12–17, 50–55
Cultwatch, 29–37

D

Delporte, Charline, 81–82, 85
deprogramming, 87, 100
doctrine, as step in conversion process, 27
Dubrow-Marshall, Linda, 102–106
Dubrow-Marshall, Rod, 102–106
Durkheim, Emile, 16

E

exiting cults, methods of, 93–101, 102–106

F

faith healing, 9, 74–79
Flat Earth Society, 51, 52, 53
Followers of Christ, 74–79
France, cult ban in, 9, 80–85
Frazer, James, 16

G

Gafatar, 67, 68–71

H
Hadden, Gerry, 80–85
"halo effect," 54
Harrison, Marye, 38–43
Hegel, George, 16
Hexham, Irving, 12–17, 15
Honigseim, P., 57
Hubbard, L. Ron, 83

I
Idaho, and faith healing, 9, 73–79
Ikeda, Daisaku, 40, 42
indoctrination/recruitment, methods of, 8, 9, 18–23, 24–28, 45–49, 50–55, 61–66
Indonesia, ban on cults in, 9, 67–71
International Church of Christ, 62
invite, as step in conversion process, 25

J
James, William, 16
Jehovah's Witnesses, 8, 24–28, 59, 81, 82
Jones, Jim, 22
Jonestown, 8, 19, 87

K
Kant, Immanuel, 16
Koresh, David, 23, 70

L
Layton, Carolyn, 19
London Church of Christ, 63

M
Manson, Charles, 8, 89
Marx, Karl, 16
mass suicide, 8, 19, 83
Mayer, R., 58
McKay, David, 25
Meepagala, Ruwan, 50–55
Milford, Stanley, 22
Moore, Annie, 19
Moore, Rebecca, 18–23
Mori, Christine, 84, 85
Mormons, 8, 24–28
motivational interviewing, 104

N
narrative, as step in conversion process, 26
new religious movements, cults as, 9, 12–17, 86–92
nonreligious cults, 8

O
Order of the Solar Temple, 83
Oregon, legislation regarding faith healing in, 75

P
Pentecostal Protestantism, 81
Peoples Temple, 19, 22
purpose, as step in conversion process, 26–27

R
Ropi, Ismatu, 67–71
Ross, Rick, 93–101
Roux, Eric, 83
Russell, Charles, 26

S
Schleiermacher, Friedrich, 16
Scientology, 8, 45–49, 65–66, 81, 83
sects, overview of types of, 12–17, 56–60
sense of community, as reason for joining cults, 24–28
Singleton, Andrew, 45–49
Smart, Ninian, 17
Smith, Joseph, 26
Soka Gakkai International (SGI), 38–43
Sottile, Leah, 73–79
Stanford Prison Experiment, 22
Stark, Rodney, 13, 14, 15
supernatural assumptions, and religious belief, 13

T
Theory of Religion, A, 13
Thomas, Michael, 24–28

U
untestable hypothesis, 20

W
Weber, Max, 16
Whitehead, Alfred North, 16

Picture Credits

Cover T.C. Malhotra/Hulton Archive/Getty Images; p. 11 PeopleImages/E+/Getty Images; p. 14 snapgalleria/Shutterstock.com; p. 20 Lavender Bat/Shutterstock.com; p. 26 Hero Images/Getty Images; p. 31 Matej Kastelic/Shutterstock.com; p. 40 Marcos Mesa Sam Wordley/Shutterstock.com; p. 44 Bride Lane Library/Popperfoto/Getty Images; p. 47 Ted Soqui/Corbis News/Getty Images; p. 52 leolintang/Shutterstock.com; p. 57 Timothy OLeary/Shutterstock.com; p. 63 Jacob Lund/Shutterstock.com; p. 69 Goh Chai Hin/AFP/Getty Images; p. 72 mark reinstein/Shutterstock.com; p. 75 EyesWideOpen/Getty Images; p. 82 Jeff Greenberg/Universal Images Group/Getty Images; p. 88 Spencer Platt/Getty Images; p. 95 Brooks Kraft/Sygma/Getty Images; p. 104 Jupiterimages/Photolibrary/Getty Images.

Photo Researcher: Sherri Jackson